THE EARL'S HOYDEN

MADELINE MARTIN

OLIVERHEBERBOOKS

PROLOGUE

JANUARY 1, 1810, DEVON, ENGLAND, LADY
FINCH'S FINISHING SCHOOL

The old longcase clock on the landing of Lady Finch's Finishing School chimed the start of 1810 with a tinkle of magic.

Miss Hannah Bexley, the only child of the doting Baron and Baroness Westwich, tucked her chilled toes beneath her as she eagerly sat upright and glanced around at her roommates. In the year they'd been together at Lady Finch's, they'd become inseparable. So it only made sense that they would each announce their resolutions for the coming year together.

The beginning of a new year was the opportunity to reinvent oneself—a chance in which Hannah was always in sore need. If only she could make her hair less red or her freckles disappear. Sadly, she lacked any control over those aspects of her life. Of what she could alter, however, there were still many things to fix.

She considered the leather-bound journal in her hands, stamped with leaves and flowers that were dyed in shades of green and blue as they crawled elegantly around the border. It had been a gift from her parents several months back for her fifteenth birthday. Lacking anything else to do with it, she and her friends had filled the cream-colored pages with their dreams and secrets. Now they would add their 1810 resolutions.

Perhaps this year, Hannah could talk less. Or laugh a little more softly. She could be dainty and elegant in a way she never had been before. Or maybe follow the rules more precisely.

But even as the silence of the room fell upon them, it didn't lie with gentle comfort over Hannah as it did the others. No, the quiet pressed on her with an urgency to fill the gap of nothing with…well, something.

"Clearly, Lucy's resolution will not be punctuality," Hannah teased.

There went the chance to talk less.

The other three young women looked toward Lucy's empty bed in the large room the five of them shared and giggled.

"Maybe she's with Lady Alison, selecting ribbons for class." Jillian pinned her dark waves with a pinch of her fingers as if it were a bow, then gave a wry twist to her lips.

A cackle erupted from Hannah at such a thought as their dear Lucy in the clutches of the dreadfully spoiled Lady Alison. Hannah clapped her hand over her mouth to stifle the unladylike guffaw.

Laughing more quietly was now off the list as well.

Drat.

"Hopefully, she didn't take a tumble." Elizabeth cast a glance toward the door, worry in her pale blue eyes. While she moved with the grace of a dancer, she somehow managed to trip over every loose stone and bump into every low-hanging eave.

"I'll wager she's up to no good." Amy frowned. Her blonde hair was knotted up in rag rolls that bounced about on her head as she spoke.

This, of course, only made Hannah giggle more.

And Amy most likely was not wrong. Lucy was always into some kind of trouble.

At that exact moment, the door swung open, and Lucy sauntered in, her nightgown whispering about her ankles. She tossed her head back to clear a length of dark hair from her hazel eyes and grinned at them all. "I thought this would make our resolutions a little more interesting." From behind her back, she withdrew a corked bottle.

Hannah leapt to her feet, leaving the journal, and ran toward Lucy with a squeal of delight.

So much for being dainty and elegant…

"I don't think we should have that in our room." Even as Amy spoke with her usual caution, she slid from her bed to examine Lucy's prize, her curiosity piqued. "Where did you get it?"

Brandy.

"From ole Gibbons's private stash that he keeps behind the sofa." Lucy wiggled the bottle, and liquid sloshed inside.

No one ever used the ruffled pink sofa with the over-fluffed cushions. No one, that was, except the butler who needed a nip from time to time to deal with "the infernal racket of so many girls" as he groused in an audible mutter at least once a day.

"And don't fret." Lucy pointed a finger at Elizabeth. "I left him a few coins to cover a new bottle of an even finer vintage than this."

Elizabeth gave a bright smile of appreciation.

"What does it take to get drunk?" Jillian asked, peering around Hannah.

Amy narrowed her eyes at the bottle. "I wager it's about seventeen jacks. Divided between the five of us, that's exactly—"

"Now is not the time for such equations." Lucy pulled the cork free, and the hollow thunk filled the room. "We'll find out." She sniffed the contents and recoiled. "I imagine not much." With that, she put the bottle to her lips and tilted her head back. She grimaced and lowered the brandy as she wheezed out a pained exhale.

"I think you're supposed to sip it," Jillian mused.

"I've never been a rule follower," Lucy ground out and passed the bottle to Hannah. "And neither have you."

The glass was cool against Hannah's palms. "I ought to take offense to that."

"But you won't," Lucy replied, her husky voice restored.

While Lucy wasn't wrong, she wasn't entirely right either. Unlike her wayward friend, Hannah didn't intentionally break the rules. Just as she didn't intentionally talk too much or try to be overly loud.

It all sort of happened.

She didn't bother to sniff the bottle as Lucy had, or her courage might falter. No, she set aside her reservations and tossed back a mouthful.

In for a penny, in for a pound…

And like that, her last option for a New Year's resolution—

following the rules better—slipped away. Or, was swallowed away, as it were.

The liquid hit her throat like punishment, all fire and hell and awfulness. She swallowed it down so as not to spit it out and felt as though she were breathing out flames as she wheezed an exhale similar to Lucy's.

Amy immediately set to patting Hannah's back.

"Is it really that bad?" Elizabeth asked, wide-eyed, stepping away from the offending spirits.

Jillian took the bottle in a show of her own special defiance and drank. Of the three, only she did not sputter but instead offered a shrug. "Not bad."

She regarded their faces, then burst into a laugh, succumbing to a hacking cough, her green eyes watering. "But not good either," she rasped.

Amy ran to her and gently thwacked her back until Jillian waved her off, still laughing.

"Let's get to our resolutions before any one of us has to drink more of that." Jillian pointed an accusatory finger at the brandy.

Lucy tucked the bottle against her arm, and they gathered closer to the hearth. Hannah swiftly retrieved the journal, flipping to one of the back pages as she did so. She sank in the semi-circle near the fire, and heat blossomed against her icy toes and warmed the front of her nightdress.

As they settled on the plush salmon-pink carpet, Hannah already could predict each of their resolutions, even as she handed the journal to Elizabeth. Amy dipped the quill in ink for her and held it at the ready, poised over the small metal well.

"I vow to be less clumsy this year," Elizabeth said. "Or at least not be so intolerably awkward about it."

Amy cast her a sympathetic look and gave her the prepared quill.

Elizabeth scratched her vow onto a fresh page with "1810" written atop it. Hannah had written the year earlier in anticipation of the evening, her penmanship so careful and perfect, even the stern-faced Miss Cuthbert wouldn't have cause for complaint.

"And you, Amy?" Hannah asked, already guessing the answer as Amy accepted the book.

Amy gently blew at the page to dry the ink. "I would like to be kind always."

"You *are* always kind," Lucy groaned in exasperation.

Even Amy rolled her eyes at this, albeit playfully and wrote the resolution in her neat, looping script.

"And I resolve…" Lucy indulged in another gulp of brandy with only a wince this time.

"To be as wicked as possible," they all finished for her in chorus.

She blinked in surprise as they all laughed. "Apparently, I ought to resolve to be less predictable."

"Don't you dare," Elizabeth said with a giggle. "We'd be at a loss as to what to do with you."

Lucy grinned and drank from the bottle again.

All eyes turned on Hannah.

Well, the year wasn't exactly starting on fine footing, considering how many potential resolutions she'd already blundered within the short side of an hour. She sighed. "To be more patient."

"Isn't that what you tried last year?" Amy asked gently.

Lucy scoffed. "And only made it a week if I recall."

Immediately Hannah regretted having shared this information with her friends. Perhaps she truly *did* talk too much. "To be fair, patience *does* take a while," she protested.

Lucy tilted her head at the point well made.

And patience *did* take a long while to master. An eternity.

Time stretched before Hannah, dreadfully dull and hopelessly bleak. But still, she held onto the thought that patience might eventually be the key to everything she needed.

Her answer officially written beneath Lucy's scratched script, the book found its way into Jillian's hands.

Of the five of them, Jillian's answer would be the most difficult to predict. Much like the young woman herself.

One never knew what thoughts danced about behind her crystal-green eyes. She saw the world in a different hue of light, her thoughts like winding tendrils that concocted insights no one might otherwise consider.

"I resolve..." She brushed the page with a tapered finger. "To never wed."

The girls all sucked in a breath. Well, except Lucy, who snorted an unladylike laugh.

"What?" Elizabeth gasped.

Jillian's chin lifted slightly, and she got that dreamy look on her face as when a notion struck her. "What if none of us ever wed? We wouldn't have to cede ourselves or our property to a man. We wouldn't be forced into a poorly matched union with a disagreeable man."

"I don't want to wed either," Lucy said with a derisive scoff.

"Perhaps we could all live on a country estate together when we become spinsters, and our parents have given up on us," Jillian said slowly as the idea came to her. "And we can make the ballroom into an extra library stacked to the ceiling with books."

"Oh, yes," Elizabeth breathed.

Hannah's heartbeat quickened at the idea of living in the country forever. To think of never having to fret over the disinterested stares of the opposite sex again or bear the suffocating rules of society.

She was to have her debut in several years, she knew. And she did not wish to. It would be far better to enter her first season with no expectations of a match, secure in the knowledge that she would never wed.

"I shouldn't like to wed either," she said, grabbing Lucy's bottle for another searing drink. Her head was already spinning, not only from the blazing alcohol but also the freedom of never having to worry about marriage.

Or, rather, the rejection that would lead to her inability to wed. For that was her biggest fear, more than a disagreeable man to marry; it was the very real possibility of there being no man at all willing to have her as his wife.

A smile brightened Jillian's face as she wrote on a fresh page—*The Vow of the Wallflowers* with the *s* blooming into a perfectly drawn rose. Beneath that, she wrote, "The wallflowers who will take their freedom and never wed." She signed, then passed the journal to Lucy, who signed, and then on to Hannah.

"No man wants a wife who trips over air." Elizabeth blew at a lock of brown hair that had fallen over one eye. "And I should love that library filled with every novel ever written." She nodded firmly. "I'm in too."

"I want a curricle of my own," Hannah said. "Perhaps a phaeton."

"You'll have it," Jillian said emphatically. "And there will be a music room for Lucy with every instrument imaginable. And an art room for me, glowing with sunlight and overlooking the garden."

They all looked to Amy, whose cheeks were scarlet beneath her rag curlers. She opened her mouth, closed it and opened it again.

Though only fifteen, Amy was a woman destined for motherhood. She was exactly the sort who could tolerate shrieks and cries of infants with a pleasant disposition and was filled with sweet patience that even a saint would covet.

"You don't have to sign," Hannah said.

"And abandon you lot of spinsters in that manor without someone to properly look after you?" Amy reached for the book and added her signature, one she had practiced to loopy perfection. "Besides, I should like to bake confections in a kitchen without judgement."

"Then it is done." Jillian folded the book closed, sat back on her heels and beamed at them all. "None of us will ever marry."

"Wallflowers to the end." With that, Hannah helped herself to one last sip of brandy, secure in a future she could finally face.

1

JANUARY 1816, SKIPTON, ENGLAND

Hannah opened the old leather journal from her days at Lady Finch's Finishing school and touched the paper where the signatures from The Vow of the Wallflowers were written in five different scripts. The opposite page was dotted with ink as well, imprinted there all those years ago when the book was closed too quickly before the ink had fully dried.

And sealed all their fates with it. Thank heavens!

"Hannah," her mother's voice came from the other side of her bedroom door, pitching higher on the last syllable.

Hannah shrank deeper into the plushness of her bed, wishing it would swallow her up. Her maid, Mary, had delivered the message her parents desired to speak to her half an hour ago. It was not difficult to know what they wished to discuss with the start of the season looming ever closer.

Preparations to depart their country estate would begin sooner than later. Gone would be the days of ambling about in hardy boots and breathing in the crisp morning air during walks. There would be no driving her own carriage or reading up in trees with her legs dangling over the rough branches.

She would be back in shoes that pinched her toes, her hair pinned and curled, enduring insufferable niceties with people her parents wanted her to meet and gowns that made breathing difficult. Desperation welled up inside her, threatening to overwhelm her.

"Did Mary not tell you we want an audience with you?" her mother persisted from the other side of the door.

That startled Hannah upright. "She did. I...fell asleep. Forgive me."

She could hardly allow her dearest Mary to suffer because of her own disinclination to be subjected to this awful discussion. Again.

With a huff, she pushed up from the bed, nudging the old journal under her pillow as she did so. A weight settled on her shoulders like a cloak as she went to her door.

Lady Westwich's smiling face met her. "Ah, my beautiful daughter. I'm well aware of how much you dread this, but it must be done."

"Perhaps it would be advantageous to forego it this year?" Hannah suggested hopefully. "After all, I've been well informed from our previous discussions, and I—"

The tuck of her mother's lips downward stifled her futile argument.

Hannah's shoulders drooped in defeat. It would be better simply to have the arduous chat and be done. Resigned, she followed her mother down the curving staircase into the library, where the family spent most of their time. A roaring fire crackled in the hearth, beating back the worst of the winter's chill. It had been an extraordinarily cold winter and had even snowed several times.

But now was not the time for thinking of the crunching of snow beneath her boots or how it dusted the world like finely sifted powder. Now was for enduring the worst lecture of the year.

Lord Westwich looked up from the high-backed sofa by the hearth. "Ah, our darling daughter."

"Your only daughter." Hannah approached and sank into the plush chair she favored on the nights she whiled the hours away with a good book, a habit she'd picked up from Elizabeth.

"Our only child." His dark blue eyes, so like her own, met her mother's and they both frowned.

And here it came…

"Which is why we want to see you wed," Lady Westwich began.

Hannah sighed. "No one will have me."

"Because you do not present yourself." Her father waved for her mother to sit beside him, and she did as he bade, a force united.

Hannah clenched her back teeth and steeled herself for the onslaught.

"You befriend men, but not in a manner which encourages their romantic interest," her mother said gently.

Ah, and the pontification of her failings with Lord Ranford. It was a low blow to open with.

They must be desperate.

"If you're referring to Lord Ranford," Hannah said curtly. "He was disinclined to see me as anything more than a friend." She dropped her attention to her hands in her lap to prevent her parents from seeing how much the truth of her words still pulled at her.

Yes, she'd vowed never to wed years ago, but Lord Ranford had created an eagerness to see him whenever they parted. She had dared to hope…

No. She had been foolish even to bother.

And she wouldn't do so now. Not again.

It was far better to think of a spinster's estate in the country with her friends than winding another inevitable path toward a wounded heart.

"A friendship can always blossom into something more," the baroness said with a note of saccharine optimism.

"Your mother would be an exceptional grandmother." Her father smiled at her mother, besotted in a way that always made Hannah turn away with a wrinkled nose.

Her mother didn't notice Hannah's disgust, too distracted by her father's adoration. "And your father would be an exceptional grandfather."

This was truly intolerable. It was one thing to suffer through her failings in securing a husband. It was entirely another to be forced to witness her parents' open affection for one another.

Hannah's gaze slid toward the window.

Was the weather fine for riding?

As she'd hoped, it was still a beautiful day with the sun gleaming high in a clear blue sky.

"We want marriage for you," her mother went on. "And grandchildren for us."

Movement in the tree near the window caught Hannah's attention. A fluff of gray wriggled on a branch.

"London is not to your preference, we know," her mother continued. "But if you fall in love with a man—"

"One with a good name," her father interjected.

Hannah craned her neck. Was it a kitten?

"Yes, of course," her mother agreed. "A man of wealth with a good name. Then you can retire to the country as often as he allows."

It wasn't a kitten exactly, but a very small cat. The poor creature opened its pink mouth in a silent mewl, its claws scrambling on the bark of a limb far too slender.

Hannah sat upright.

"Are you listening, child?" Lady Westwich asked.

"There's a cat outside," Hannah said plaintively. "I think it needs help."

"Hannah." Her father's voice was stern with disapproval.

The animal's tail spun and flexed forward in its attempt to gain purchase. Needle-like nails raked against the branch, and it cried out once more. It was going to fall.

"We have funded your pursuit for three seasons now without result," Lord Westwich continued. "Not even one suitor has called upon me."

The cat was going to slip if Hannah didn't do something. Being so little, surely, the tumble would be an awfully long way down.

"Hannah, are you listening?" her mother demanded, her voice sharp with dwindling patience.

"I am undesirable." Hannah finally turned her attention to her parents. "I'm too much of too many things and not enough of others. I've made my peace with being a spinster. Perhaps you ought to as well."

A glance toward the window showed the cat now clinging

on by only one scrawny front leg. Her heart jumped into her throat, and she lurched to her feet.

"Please do excuse me." With that, she tore from the room in a most unladylike manner that sent her skirts whipping up around her knees and her slippers skidding over the silk carpets.

Her mother called out behind her, that blasted octave on the last part of Hannah's name trailing after her as she raced to save the poor defenseless cat from certain death. Thankfully, the butler was used to Hannah's impetuous behavior and effortlessly darted from her path as she flew by.

"Mind the carpet, Miss Bexley," he said in his bored drawl. "It slips."

"Thank you, Jones," she called out as she bounded like a dancer over the confounded thing.

If he replied, she didn't hear as she was already pushing through the door, out into the bright sunshine, ice-cold and crisp with the earthy fragrance of nature. The chill did not touch her despite lacking a coat, not with such urgency forcing her onward.

She rounded the corner with precision as the tree came into view and picked up her pace.

The cat squirmed, the little limb no longer strong enough to support its weight, and it dropped. Hannah screamed and held out her skirt in a final bid to save the poor thing.

It landed with a plop that tugged at her dress, but she caught it. There was a moment where their eyes met in mutual surprise, her in shock that she had actually managed to secure it in the drape of her skirt, and it to be in such a peculiar situation as a lady's skirts.

Before Hannah could even register that she was standing in the middle of the lawn with her hem pulled to her knees, the cat hopped from the hammock of her skirt and darted off. A small smear of blood remained on the white muslin of her day dress.

It was hurt.

"Wait," she shouted, as if the creature would listen.

It didn't and continued to bound through the high, straw-like winter grass with fervor. But Hannah was not so easily deterred.

She dashed after the little beast, amazed at its haste with an apparent injury. Time in the country always did her considerable good—the fresh air and long walks helpful for building her stamina in anticipation of long nights of dancing through the season—but as she ran and ran and ran, her energy began to wane.

It was only the thought of an injured animal left to the cruelties of nature that spurred her faster.

A fence appeared in the distance. It was simple, with horizontal slats framed by thick wooden posts. Of course, the kitten darted toward it, ducking underneath while Hannah was left to scale the structure. As she neared, she discovered it was taller than anticipated. There would be nothing for it but to climb.

With her gaze locked on the dot of gray fur racing from her, she placed one foot on the lower beam, her hands clutching the wood that splintered against her palms. Then she clambered higher to the next. It was on the third slat, as she was throwing her leg over the other side, when the support beneath her gave a definitive and ominous crack.

All at once, her footing disappeared, and she pitched

forward, arms spiraling helplessly into the air as she flopped on the other side of the fence with a forceful *oof*.

Lucien Lambert, the fifth Earl of Brightstone, sought solace resting against the rough bark of an old elm tree, lost in the teachings of Aristotle where they were best appreciated—in nature. The afternoon thus far had been as Lucien anticipated, bringing an appreciation of the world around him. What he had not expected was a startling crack or a massive rat propelling itself toward his chest.

The thing landed with a resounding thud and made him jerk away hard enough that he slammed the back of his head against the aged bark. His shock quickly ebbed when he realized the animal was no rodent but instead a small gray cat. Wide blue eyes stared up at him, its tiny claws embedded into Lucien's plain brown waistcoat.

"Where the devil have you dropped in from?" Lucien remarked.

The beast scrabbled up his jacket and issued a quiet meow. He cupped the thing against his chest, mindful of those little talons. The cat's heart thumped a frantic beat against his palm. Lucien stood and looked around the tree to see what had frightened the poor animal.

There, lying beneath a newly broken slat in the fence, was a woman. Well, a rather splayed-out woman, as it were.

Her white dress was tossed up past her knees, and one woolen stocking had fallen low, revealing a slender calf. The other was stained bright red at the knee. Delicate slippers, meant more for the carpeted interior of a home rather than a dash through the country, jutted up from the grass with the blue silk toes pointed toward the sky.

Lucien rushed to her as she pushed onto her elbows, her expression bewildered beneath a tangle of lovely red curls, revealing her to be his neighbor, Miss Bexley. They had briefly met when they were children, a lifetime ago, and he'd seen her at several social events through the years.

But this was the first time he'd been so close to her as an adult. She was rather becoming, with a generous mouth that quirked up at the corners and dark-lashed, sparkling blue eyes.

He extended his free hand. "Allow me to help you up."

She did not accept his help and instead pulled at the fabric of her skirt to cover her naked legs. "Look away," she gasped. "Please."

He spun about quickly, putting his back to her, the cat still cupped in his hand. "Forgive me, Miss Bexley. I merely wanted to assist you to your feet. I didn't mean to be untoward."

"No, of course you didn't, my lord," she replied hurriedly. There was a slight rustle of fabric, and when she spoke again, she was directly behind him. "It is I who should beg your forgiveness. I didn't mean to be so abrupt. I...I was quite taken aback by your sudden arrival before I could put myself to rights."

He turned to find her standing upright. The knot holding her hair up was so loose, tendrils streamed down her flushed face in a most enticing manner. Her legs were covered once more with a white muslin dress ruined by streaks of green from her tumble. A spot of red had begun to show near her knee.

"You're hurt." He frowned. "And you haven't a coat." Immediately, he shrugged out of his. Or he began to, that is. The feat was not easily managed when he had only one hand to work with, as the other still held the cat.

She shook her head even as he wrestled out of the garment. "Please, I assure you, I'm quite warm from having chased the cat."

"This cat?" Lucien asked as he continued to struggle with his coat, refusing to allow a lady to stand in a day dress in the middle of a frigid field without a coat. Finally, he freed it from his person and awkwardly draped it over her shoulders with her help.

A peppery sensation prickled deep in his nose. Soon there would be sneezing, followed by the inability to breathe properly. No doubt his eyes would well up, becoming an itchy red a moment after that.

Oh misery, what had inspired him to pick up the animal?

But then, it hadn't given him much of a choice, had it?

At that moment, however, with the euphoric gleam in Miss Bexley's eyes as she gazed at him as one did an unquestioning hero, he was glad to have helped the animal. Sinus misery and all.

"I see you found him." She approached Lucien and reached up for the kitten, stroking its small face.

The creature lifted its head to present its small chin as a delicate rumble began in its chest.

Lucien couldn't help but chuckle. "He found me."

Miss Bexley looked at him with a winning laugh, her striking eyes as blue as a cloudless summer sky.

Everything about her was bold and vibrant, from the brilliance of her hair to the glow of her personality.

"I thought I would never catch him." She glanced back at the fence, and her cheeks flushed deep red as she put her palm to her brow in a display of forgetfulness. "What a mess I am. First breaking your fence, then appearing in such an inappropriate fashion." She shook her head. "My mother would be terribly disappointed in me."

The lightness of her tone suggested her mother would not be happy, of course, but likely wouldn't truly be disappointed in her. Not like Lucien's mother so often was with him.

"It truly is no trouble at all on my part," he said. The tickling in his nose left his eyes tingling.

His mother had much to say about Miss Bexley—namely that she was loud and impertinent, a true hoyden if ever Lady Brightstone had seen one. And while the circumstances of his reunion with Miss Bexley did suggest a certain undeniable impulsivity on her part, there was something radiant about her that appealed greatly to him.

He handed her the cat. "Your pet is safe."

She accepted the puff of gray fur with a demure nod. "I will ensure my father's man has your fence mended."

"I worry more after your injury," he admitted, indicating the growing stain of blood on her dress.

"It's nothing." She gave a laugh and waved away his worry.

There was a light carelessness about her that made him want to know more about her. She wasn't as stiff and formal and difficult to read as other women of the ton. He tried to recall her personality as a child and could not, remembering only a smattering of freckles and messy hair.

Hoyden or not, she seemed kind, and she was friendly. Both were recommendations he could not make of most women in society.

"I believe you lost your hat," he said. "Perhaps it is with your coat?"

"Oh." Her hand clapped onto her mussed hair.

"I can help you locate them," he said, suddenly anxious to keep their conversation going, no matter how stilted it might be.

"I didn't...or rather, I wasn't wearing them," she stammered. "I ran out of the house so quickly, as the cat was slipping from the tree, there wasn't a spare moment to put them on. However, I did manage to catch him with my skirt." She startled suddenly and looked down at her skirt where a small smear of reddish-brown showed. "The poor dear is wounded."

"You are as well, Miss Bexley."

She paid him no mind as she pried one little paw to inspect before moving on to the next. With a soft tsk, she leaned over the cat. She was so near to Lucien that the sweet, citrusy scent of her perfume teased at his awareness.

Miss Bexley gazed up at him and batted her wide blue eyes. "May I?" She could have asked him for his entire library at that moment and he might have given it up.

Or perhaps not.

He *was* quite fond of his collection of philosophical works.

Rather than try to flounder for something witty to remark upon or perhaps ask what it was she wanted, he simply nodded.

No sooner had his head moved than his handkerchief was whisked from his coat pocket and wrapped around the creature's wounded paw.

"And what of your injury?" he inquired, unable to let her bleeding knee go, especially when the stain on her dress seemed to bloom larger by the second.

"Oh, it's fine." She shrugged a shoulder at his concern. "Truly. It isn't the first injury I've sustained, nor will it likely be my last. I'm sure you've heard I'm something of a hoyden."

Her blatant remark surprised him as it was uncommon for a woman to be so forthright. It was quite refreshing.

"Does it bother you?" The abruptness of his question was confirmed by the way her head snapped toward him.

An impending sneeze prickled at the back of his nose. He exhaled slowly to quell the urge.

Her slim brows lifted, the same fiery red as her hair. "Does being a hoyden bother me?"

Before he could stammer out an excuse to cover his awkward inquiry, Miss Bexley answered her question. "It's who I am."

She flashed a smile at him and cradled the kitten to her. "Though I do suppose my mother will be rather put out with me for ruining another gown."

A polite glance at her day dress confirmed it was indeed ruined. It was the only part of the encounter that appeared to leave Miss Bexley distressed. That and the fence, of course.

The desperate urge to sneeze attacked him again, welling in his eyes and tingling at the back of his nose. "You can tell your mother it was my fault," he suggested.

To his surprise, Miss Bexley laughed, a light, silvery sound that rose unabashed in a world where ladies quietly giggled behind hands and fans. The surprise of it thankfully shocked away his need to sneeze.

"I can imagine saying as much to my mother would put me in far greater trouble. And you too." She tilted her head, considering him for a moment. "But I truly do appreciate the offer, Lord Brightstone."

The cat squirmed in her hands. "I'll have my father's man see to your fence. Thank you again for not being cross with me over its destruction."

"You needn't worry," he rushed, not wanting her to upset her parents further. "I'll have the fence repaired before you can even notify your father."

She chewed on her bottom lip, clearly warring with herself before turning her sunny smile upon him once more. "Thank you. Truly. And for also saving Leaf."

"Leaf?"

She stroked a hand over the animal's small furry head. "Since he fell from a tree, the name only seemed fitting."

It was a whimsical name for a cat, but one that somehow fit with this fascinating woman's stream of consciousness. "Indeed, it does."

"It was good to see you again after all this time." Miss Bexley gave a little curtsey.

Lucien smiled at her. "The pleasure was all mine." And truly, it was.

"Oh, your coat." She gracefully swirled it from her shoulders with one hand and extended it to him. "Thank you for your chivalry."

He accepted the garment. "Of course."

With one last smile, she spun from him, cat in hand, and strode away without limping. Lucien waited as she strolled away, his eyes watering until she was out of sight, when he could finally yield to his tremendous urge with a great and unfettered sneeze.

⁓

ONLY WHEN HANNAH was entirely certain Lord Brightstone was out of sight did she allow herself to limp. After the excitement of her accident and the energy charging in her system as she'd chased little Leaf ebbed away, the sting of her injury made itself known. As did the biting cold.

She hadn't realized how much of a chill the wind held until she swept the heat of his coat from her shoulders to return it to him. There had been a pleasant smell to the coat—shaving soap, the familiar aroma of books and an underlying spice.

"I'm grateful you are safe," she said to Leaf.

It nuzzled closer to her, purring furiously where she cradled the warm puff against her bosom, completely heedless of her limp.

"It was kind of Lord Brightstone to save you," she continued. "And to be so gracious about his broken fence."

Mortification washed over her at her folly, at the way her skirts had flipped up with her graceless tumble.

"And my indecency," she added miserably to the uninterested cat.

What was more, he had not regarded her with the bewildered horror he should have, which most certainly would have.

No, Lord Brightstone had been understanding and gracious, almost appearing somewhat flustered himself.

She recalled him well from of the few times they'd been in one another's company in her youth. He'd never wanted to climb trees or catch frogs in the streams, preferring instead to sequester himself in the vast silence of the library. Hannah loved books as well, an appreciation she'd garnered at Elizabeth's enthusiastic behest, but Hannah never could bring herself to be as quiet as the room warranted.

The years had been good to Lord Brightstone. He was now a handsome man with blue eyes that possessed an undeniable keenness. Granted, his wavy blond hair was several weeks overdue for a trim, and a slight shadow of whiskers over his strong jaw suggested he hadn't bothered to shave that morning. Even his clothes appeared somewhat disorderly and rumpled. She rather liked the lack of airs he took on in the country, being so much like herself.

When away from London, she could set aside the discomforts of society fashion. She far preferred comfortable attire as she reveled in her freedom in the open fields and endless forests amid the wildly beautiful allure of nature.

As she limped toward the house, she already anticipated the theatrics of her mother's reaction. Suddenly, Hannah was immensely grateful to Lord Brightstone for his offer to have his man fix the fence. The less her parents knew of her humiliation, the better.

In fact, she could pretend as though the entire meeting had never happened. If Lady Westwich knew Hannah had been speaking to the earl next door, the baroness would surely attribute far more to the meeting than need be. The last thing Hannah wanted as she was propelled into another fruitless season was to be shoved in Lord Brightstone's direction.

2

From the warm comfort of his library, Lucien gazed out at the field near the elm tree where he'd been speaking to Hannah. His groundskeeper strolled toward the broken fence, the length of wood for a new slat tucked against the man's side.

The prickling of an itchy throat and watery eyes had finally abated after Lucien scrubbed at his face and changed his attire. But it wasn't physical discomfort that lodged itself in his thoughts.

It was her.

Miss Bexley.

The intrepid saver of cats, unusual in a markedly exciting manner. Beautiful and radiant.

"What is amiss with the fence?" A stern voice at Lucien's side inquired.

He turned to find his mother staring hawkishly at the groundskeeper with a steely gray gaze that missed nothing and found everything wanting. A beam of sunlight shone through the windows, stopping short of her slippered feet as if too afraid to approach her.

"I believe the wood rotted," Lucien replied easily. It wouldn't do at all to inform his mother of how Miss Bexley had climbed over the slat, snapping the wood before tumbling to the ground with her skirt flung up to her knees.

Pretty knees though they were—or at least the uninjured one with the fallen stocking. Granted, he was no scoundrel and hadn't ogled her in her precarious state. But neither was he a saint. And her legs were far too fine to ignore, long and slender, yet perfectly shaped with a sensual curve at her calf and ankle.

"Rotten wood?" Lady Brightstone echoed with a frown. "It was redone last year."

He gave a non-committal shrug and returned his gaze to the book in front of him.

"I saw you speaking to that Bexley chit," his mother said in a tone that was anything but casual.

"You mean Miss Bexley," he corrected.

Lady Brightstone harrumphed. "Have I told you that Lady Townsend is in a delicate way?"

Lucien reread the page and hummed a response that presented no opinion at all. This was merely a catalyst for a conversation they often had.

"She already has three children, two boys and a girl," Lady Brightstone continued. "One can only imagine being blessed with so many grandchildren."

It was beyond Lucien why his mother wished for grandchildren when she had scarcely abided him as a child.

"Are you suggesting I make a bid for Miss Bexley's hand to

procure several grandchildren for you?" Even as Lucien spoke, he couldn't help the curious little thrill of his words.

"Oh heavens, of course not." His mother put her hand to her chest as though the very idea was enough to send her into an apoplectic fit. "She's far too provincial to be with a Lambert. But she could be good practice."

Lucien narrowed his eyes at the sly tone to Lady Brightstone's nasally drawl. "I fail to understand what you mean."

She waved her hand airily. "You could flirt with her. Have her be a whetstone to sharpen your wit upon."

"My wit is plenty sharp," Lucien muttered. It was perhaps too much so, which set him apart from those around him in an awkward, uncomfortable manner.

"Your wit is dry," his mother corrected. "And it isn't as though you would have competition. No one else has shown interest in the hoyden for three seasons. I'd thought perhaps Lord Ranford might take the plunge, but she likely scared him off with all her chatter. Or that raucous laugh."

"I haven't paid attention to how other's seasons transpire," he replied truthfully. There were far too many comings and goings of this or that person's interest in the span of a single night to give their activities more than a passing thought, let alone keeping track of an entire season.

"She seems like the kind of girl to gossip." Lady Brightstone pursed her lips. "A busybody always in everyone else's business."

Lucien arched a brow at his mother's scowl. "How very ironic."

She shot him a long-suffering glare, apparently catching his meaning. "You must wed, Lucien, to have an heir. No matter the cost."

A distant banging sounded outside, muted by the windows. The repairs were officially underway.

"I refuse to obtain a wife by using another eligible woman as practice," Lucien retorted.

"Eligible." His mother scoffed and needlessly adjusted the deep blue puff of one velvet sleeve. The thing looked overlarge on her thin arms.

"Miss Bexley is a kind and honest lady." He closed his book and gave his mother a sharp look. The world might cower at her feet, but he was not that kind of man. "I will not hurt her to appease you."

"You need a wife, and you need an heir," she replied vehemently. "I don't care how you procure a reasonable lady to acquire them."

If his parents' marriage was any indication of how wedded life could be, it was no wonder he'd never applied himself in the pursuit of a bride. The former Earl of Brightstone had skulked around his wife, desperate to be free of her waspish ways, often finding solace in the arms of various women. Though he had been discreet, Lady Brightstone was well aware of these indiscretions, which had only made the acid of her verbal assaults all the more potent.

But while Lucien would take a life of solace and books over such marital torment, he knew his mother was correct. He would need to wed eventually, regardless of his disinclination to do so. It was, after all, his duty to produce the next Earl of Brightstone.

"Ladies are uninterested in me." It was a dull argument, but one he was comfortable falling back on. After all, none of those ladies had interested him either.

"Then you need to address why they are not." His mother indicated his person. "Look at you, wearing a plain yellow waistcoat when blue would bring out your eyes. And your hair flopping about in your face. You were lucky enough to inherit my cheekbones." She paused to delicately stroke the elegant line of her face. "You ought to let them be seen."

His mother was far too attentive to her appearance. Her blue day dress was adorned with a costly brooch and matching earbobs, despite a lack of visitors to their country estate since the former earl's death. Regardless, every morning she rose with the sun and insisted her maid scrape her silver-and-gold hair back into a high chignon with exactly six sausage-like curls framing her face.

He sighed. "I don't need to primp myself to be put on display, mother."

"Why not?" she demanded. "Women are expected to do so, as are men."

"I'm hardly a popinjay." He scanned the scores of books behind his mother, eager to lose himself in their edifying embrace once more. Honestly, he'd rather subject himself in the scribbling of a dilettante's attempts at poetry than endure this conversation for much longer.

His mother issued a harsh laugh. "You assuredly are not. But you could at least apply yourself. What about that Bexley hoyden next door?"

Lucien didn't bother to suppress his sigh. "Miss Bexley," he corrected.

Again.

"She may be far too brash for my liking, but she does have a good eye for fashion." Lady Brightstone's lips pinched as if the grudging praise caused her a physical ache. "If nothing else, you could at least ask her for advice on what to wear. Since you refuse to accept any of the gentle suggestions I've offered." She sniffed with indignity.

In the past, her "gentle suggestions" were delivered with the delicacy of a bruiser's right hook.

Before he could brush aside this new idea, his mother continued, "And this way, you would not cause her any harm. It would merely be advice."

With that, she lifted her nose into the air and sailed abruptly from the room, no doubt counting his inability to respond as a win in favor of her argument. Her suggestion lingered in the air behind her like the fog of old perfume.

But then a strange thing happened as the memory of those words settled over him, the idea becoming less unsavory as the minutes ticked by. His mother did have a point, though Lucien would never admit it.

Surely, a discussion with Miss Bexley could guide him toward being more fashionable. Loathsome though the idea of altering his comfortable attire seemed, the enticement of conversing again with Miss Bexley was undeniably appealing.

Yes, he would do it. His decision was made at that very moment. He would seek out Miss Bexley's counsel on ways he might improve his overall appearance for the undesirable goal of securing a countess.

WHILE WINTER WAS NOT Hannah's favorite season, the trail through the woods still held a note of magic as frost glittered like fairy dust over the naked limbs of trees and over ground-level shrubs that managed to maintain some of their leaves. She inhaled, taking in the fresh air amid the scents of damp earth as the curricle rolled along the path.

Having the freedom to drive her carriage was one of the many things she loved about the country. She sat a little higher on the seat and glanced behind her to ensure the manor house was no longer in sight. Confident she wouldn't be seen, she slipped free the silk ribbon under her chin and pulled away the weight of her bonnet.

Freckles be damned. She loved the wind caressing her skin and hair as she drove.

Besides, it wasn't as though she had ever encountered anyone on this path. She'd navigated the pair of horses down its twisting curves every day of their time in Skipton for years and never came upon a single soul.

"Miss Bexley," a voice called out.

She jumped with a start and her boots—so much more practical for the country than dainty slippers—slapped upon the wooden floor. The horses jolted forward in surprise, sending her bonnet toppling over the side of the bench.

"Whoa, Bess. Whoa, Tabitha," she said in a soothing voice to the startled mares.

The velvety brown beasts calmed immediately and slowed to a stop.

Hannah swiftly leapt down from her curricle to retrieve the bonnet, her feet sinking several inches into the thick mud, and found a gentleman already bent over the headwear to retrieve it for her. Unfortunately, as he pulled it free, glops of mud and partially frozen water fell from the side that had landed directly in a slushy puddle. Bitter disappointment burned in Hannah's stomach. Mother would be livid, especially so soon after Hannah had ruined her dress.

"I'm afraid it's soiled." Lord Brightstone met her gaze with a look of genuine chagrin.

Heat washed over her cheeks. "Well, I suppose it isn't as though you've never seen me without my bonnet." She laughed at her self-deprecating comment.

"It's fortunate for you that you've such lovely hair." He extended the dripping bonnet toward her.

She accepted it in a state of shock, her gaze locked on him. Lovely hair? Usually, people called it garish. As overbright as her laugh was overloud. Yet another facet of her "too much" personality.

A blush colored his cheeks. "Should I not have said that?" He cleared his throat. "Forgive me. I don't always say the correct things."

She shook her head. "No, I…it's…you see, no one has said my hair is lovely before." She shrugged. "Well, except my mother, but of course, she doesn't count. Not only is she biased toward me, but her mother had hair this color. And my friends, of course. They have complimented it, though they, too, are rather biased. I suppose, really, no *man* has ever told me that before."

She was rambling. God help her.

Be silent, Hannah.

If he minded her wordy, pointless statement, he gave no sign of irritation.

She held the dripping bonnet in one hand, taking care to hold it away from her lest mud stained the side of her gown and ruined it as well.

How could she have been such a ninny as to remove the bonnet? She'd become too comfortable in her solitude, and now, once more, she appeared before the earl in an unladylike state. This time, she didn't even have the excuse of rescuing a cat to salvage her improper dress.

In hindsight, she ought to at least have held her bonnet on her arm by its ribbons like a reticule.

"I've been hoping to see you again," Lord Brightstone said stiffly.

He had been *hoping* to see her?

Hope flared up inside Hannah, igniting a flame in what had long since been cold ash. The sensation was irrational and impulsive and pitiful in how viscerally the need to be wanted burned inside her. And yet, she could not quash it once it flickered to life.

No matter the vow she had made with the other women at Lady Finch's Finishing School, no matter how often she told herself she did not want marriage or children or love, she craved it all.

Desperately.

He had been hoping to see her again.

"Have you?" she asked, the icy morning air suddenly too thin to inhale properly.

And how could she when the back of her mind ran down a wayward path with a speed she couldn't control?

Her imagination carried her into London ballrooms where she spun about the dancefloor in Lord Brightstone's arms, to a dinner party announcing their engagement, back to the country where they wed under a bower of fresh summer roses and on to a nursery crooning over a swaddled infant.

An ache settled in her chest, powerful and poignant. One

that couldn't be willed away no matter how preposterous she knew her musings to be. The future that had rushed to her with such immediacy was what she truly, foolishly, hopelessly wanted.

Lord Brightstone had complimented her hair, and now she had taken that pearl to make a necklace of dreams from. She was being ridiculous. Wistful in a way that was unwarranted.

"I wondered if you might…" He looked down and shook his head, as though wrestling with how to say what he intended.

Her heartbeat thundered in her ears. If she might what? Wish to be courted by him?

Had he already discussed the matter with her father?

She stepped closer to him and lowered her face slightly to catch his gaze. "Please, you can ask me anything."

He swallowed, his nervousness apparent.

"I wondered if you might," he said again. "Assist me with being more fashionable."

Her future disappeared in an instant, her hope little more than a wisp of smoke from a snuffed candle flame.

She blinked. "I beg your pardon?"

A small animal moved through the brush somewhere in the distance, setting the leaves rustling. Lord Brightstone shifted his weight from one foot to another. "My mother has been displeased with my lack of courtship. I thought perhaps you might offer some suggestions."

If Hannah's cheeks were warm before, they were on fire now.

Heavens, but she was a dolt. A daydreaming ninny who ought to know her place in this cruel society by now. "I'm hardly one to give advice in the ways of courtship as I've never had a suitor myself." Saying it aloud made the admission even more pathetic.

He rubbed a hand at the back of his neck. "My mother thinks highly of your fashion sense."

"Does she?" This conversation did not lack surprises. Hannah had always assumed Lady Brightstone detested her.

"She also thinks little of my own." His glanced down to examine his tea-colored shirt and brown waistcoat and jacket. "I am in sore need of aid." He regarded her once more, his blue eyes meeting hers beneath his overlong blond waves. "I thought perhaps you might be willing to take pity on an unfashionable wretch like me." He winced. "Without turning me into a foppish dandy, please."

Hannah had to chuckle at that. Even if she wanted to, Lord Brightstone could never become a dandy. His personality was too somber for something so bold.

"And you seem very kind." He shrugged shyly.

Kind. She almost groaned. Kindness was seemingly her one good trait as it was an attribute that she'd heard mentioned previously in regard to her person.

Other women were beautiful or talented or delicate. She was kind.

And had a good fashion sense, according to the sharp eye —and judgement—of Lady Brightstone. How could Hannah say no?

She nodded. "Of course, I can help you."

The earl released a breath of relief. "I appreciate your aid more than I can say." He held his hands out to the side, putting himself at the mercy of her assessment. "What can I do to improve?"

Hannah preferred not to look at others critically. Not

when she herself had been the subject of scrutiny for so many years. Instead, she took his words to heart to inspect what might be improved upon rather than simply stating what was wrong.

"Your hair will need a trim," she mused. Though it was regretful when his wavy locks seemed as if they would feel silky soft, and the cut seemed to fit the shape of his face. But fashion didn't care for shapes, only conformity.

Lord Brightstone chuckled. "My valet will be delighted as he's been after me about trimming my hair for at least a fortnight now."

"Your cravat can be tighter, and your shirt points higher," she suggested.

"Ah, yes." His fingertips brushed the loose bundle of silk messily pinned at his throat. "I take ownership of this faux pas as I have a penchant for loosening the thing. It always leaves me feeling as though I'm being strangled."

"Perhaps the Mail Coach might be best?" The knot was as simple as a cravat could be without any jutting fabric propelling along the sides of the neck.

"I shall inform my valet at once," Lord Brightstone vowed.

"Though you possibly will want all of your garments to be more closely fitting." She skimmed his brown jacket with her gaze and walked around him in contemplation, noting the elbows were worn nearly through. "And breeches haven't been in fashion for day wear for some time." She indicated his trousers. "Unless they're buckskin, which you would do well to procure at least one pair. Pair it with a dark wool coat, I think."

She tilted her head, imagining him dressed in the outfit and beginning to enjoy herself. "Oh, yes, very much so. Navy."

It was almost like dressing up dolls when she was a girl, but instead of a toy, her subject was a handsome grown man who would be made all the more dashing from her instruction.

"You need more tightly fit trousers and pantaloons," she said excitedly.

"Pantaloons?" Lord Brightstone wrinkled his nose. "Even the name sounds absurd."

"Yes, pantaloons. And have several jackets made in the new military fashion with blue wool or silk or velvet and gold buttons throughout. It will become you very nicely."

"Is that all?" he asked dryly.

"And a topper."

He arched a brow. Or at least she thought he did beneath his thick hair. "A topper?"

"Yes, fine silk top hats. They're grand with evening attire and with greatcoats that are also all the rage." She spoke with finality. "You definitely need a topper. And perhaps a cane."

"I can walk unaided on my own, thank you."

"Not for assistance in walking, but for show," she explained. "Or perhaps a pocket watch and fob?"

"A pocket watch would suit me. And I shall purchase a topper." He bowed to her. "Thank you for your time and for sharing your expertise."

"Of course." Hannah smiled at him, genuinely glad to have provided him counsel.

"I bid you a good day and wish you safe travels to London for the upcoming season." With that, he took his leave.

Hannah remained where she stood a moment longer, watching as he departed, her ruined bonnet at her side and her broken dreams in pieces within her heart.

London.

She and her parents were to leave the following week for the beginning of yet another season, for another opportunity to be rejected. Another reminder of her ineptitude.

At least, if nothing else, she might have offered someone else a fighting chance, even as her own was already lost.

3

FEBRUARY 1816, LONDON, ENGLAND

*L*ondon was bitterly cold and abysmally dreary. More so than usual. Hannah stood on the small stool in Madame Bannery's while the modiste moved around her in halting pauses. The woman's dark head was bent over the careful work, pins tucked neatly between her lips as she hemmed Hannah's new ballgown.

Goosebumps prickled over her bare arms, but she didn't voice her discomfort, not when Madame Bannery's girl had already added a fresh log to the fire moments before.

"I expect this will be your season, Hannah." Lady Westwich carefully inspected a length of yellow Spitalfields silk with a moss-green and royal-blue floral pattern across its edge. "I can *feel* it."

Most likely, what Lady Westwich felt was the remnants of her toast points from that morning, which never failed to give her a touch of dyspepsia.

Hannah acted as though she had not heard her mother.

"Did you hear me, Hannah?" The baroness turned pointedly to her. "This is going to be your season."

If Hannah could properly breathe in the pinned garment, she might have sighed. Fear of being stabbed by the pins holding the fabric in place, however, had her squelching the reaction.

"Yes, Mother."

Lady Westwich did sigh. "Don't patronize me with platitudes, daughter. I have it on good authority we are to be invited to the opening ball at Ranford Place." Her mother beamed, clearly proud of herself. "Lord Ranford." The man's name was said slowly, as if Hannah was simpleminded, followed by a suggested raising of the baroness's light brows.

Hannah groaned. "We are merely friends, Mother."

Madame Bannery straightened and turned Hannah to work on a piece of the small cap sleeve, breaking Lady Westwich's fixed stare.

Thank heavens!

The baroness shifted to be in front of Hannah, locking onto her gaze once more. "But you could be more than friends."

"He needed advice on Lady Julia's coming out," Hannah replied.

"It was kind of you to aid him through his sister's debut since their mother has been gone for so long, but if you pressed your advantage with him…" Lady Westwich settled a hand on Hannah's arm.

Kind.

There was that confounded word again.

"Oh, you're freezing, Hannah," her mother cried.

The shop assistant ran toward the hearth without hesitation and plunged two more logs into the flames before Hannah could even protest. However, as a blast of heat washed over her bare arms, she was grateful for a reprieve from the chill.

"What I was saying is that your friendship could blossom into something more," Lady Westwich continued, never one to be swayed from the path of dogged conversation. "Like your father and I did."

Hannah sighed and was rewarded with a sharp prick from one of the pins at her ribs.

Her mother was forever using her union with Hannah's father as a lesson in what marriage should be. The discussion was as tedious as it was off-putting with how they longingly looked at one another. The long, drawn-out stares were what young lovers were wont to do. Not self-respecting, cultured adults.

Madame Bannery gently spun Hannah around to address the other dainty sleeve.

"What about Lord Brightstone?" her mother asked.

Hannah was grateful not to be facing Lady Westwich at that moment as Hannah was sure her face flushed as vibrantly red as her hair. What could her mother possibly know about Lord Brightstone? Hannah had never divulged that she had even spoken with him.

"Our neighbor in Skipton?" Hannah hoped she sounded more innocent and aloof to her mother than she did to herself.

The baroness appeared in front of her, lips pursed, stare assessing. She knew something.

But how?

Hannah schooled her features to remain entirely impassive.

"You are finished, Miss Bexley." Madame Bannery pulled a

pin from her mouth and smiled at her—a gesture Hannah returned enthusiastically. Dressing would at least present an opportunity to escape from her mother for a few more moments.

Mary helped Hannah into several layers of clothing, topping it all with a deep lapis-blue velvet day dress.

"How does my mother know about Lord Brightstone?" Hannah whispered to her maid, who widened her eyes and shrugged.

Mary had informants throughout the Westwich staff, expertly extracting whatever information was necessary to pass on to Hannah. If she had heard something about Lord Brightstone, she would have relayed it. Whatever Lady Westwich knew, she was keeping it close to her bosom.

Which sorely vexed Hannah.

What was she in for once they were alone in the carriage? Away from the sharp ears of the modiste and shop girl, who were always keen to discover the newest juicy rumor to feed to their clients.

"Have any of your friends arrived in London yet?" Lady Westwich asked casually.

It was a ruse, a play for conversation to mask her inquiry about Lord Brightstone. The baroness was so transparent that it was practically galling. Her query as to Lord Brightstone had been merely a bid to wield gossip to stake Hannah's claim on the earl before anyone else could ready their claws that season.

Considering that he was as much of a catch as Hannah, such a move was hardly necessary.

"They never return to London as early as we do," Hannah replied baldly.

"Which you know," she added silently.

Her mother tilted her head as though the news was novel and fascinating. "I see. Well, I am sure they will return shortly, and you can be reunited."

Of everything to do with the season, the only aspect Hannah looked forward to was seeing the women she'd roomed with at the finishing school all those years ago. They'd been fast friends and remained such through their debuts, followed by the next three seasons that left them all blessedly unmatched.

Well, all of them but Jillian, that was. Her father was determined to marry her off. The first contender was a fashionable gentleman whose appearance had been more admirable than his dull wit. Though he'd doted on her when others were about, much to her consternation, his eye wandered to every lovely creature who passed. His eye had not been the only part of his person that wandered, which led to an indiscretion with another man's wife, which was his untimely demise when he found himself on the wrong end of a duel.

Then there was the Marquess of Mastronry, who had thought himself besotted with Jillian. In the end, her not-so-subtle lack of interest and her curious nature ran him into the arms of an up-and-coming debutante who was rumored to be "'in a delicate way" a fortnight prior to their hasty nuptials.

Doubtless, the season would bring another ill-fated match for poor Jillian.

Hannah didn't seem to be in a better position than her friend now if Lady Westwich had anything to do with it. Her mother guided them through the modiste's shop and toward the door. It was nearly flung off its hinges by a vicious gust of wind that came sweeping down Bond Street as they spilled out onto the walkway.

Lady Westwich sucked in a breath, as though her soul had almost been blown away.

Hannah clapped a hand on her hat, securing it against her head to keep the pins from being ripped from her scalp. Outside, their coach stood at the ready, the footman fighting to hold the door open for them.

Hannah, Mary and her mother clustered together for strength and warmth and rushed toward the carriage, climbing in as fast as was possible in a ladylike manner—if one could even consider anything ladylike while being shoved forcefully to the side by the violent wind.

The tidy blonde curls around her mother's face had been whipped about into an awkwardly jutting puff that careened to the right. "Well," she huffed. "I dare say this is the coldest winter we've seen in London." She patted her head, then paused, frowning with bewildered horror as she traced the mass of her hair upward with her gloved fingertips.

A giggle rose in Hannah's throat, which she only partially succeeded in swallowing down.

"You could at least cough, so your mirth isn't as obvious, Hannah." Her mother slid a sardonic gaze from the corner of her eye, which made Hannah laugh out loud.

One of Lady Westwich's chief attributes was her sunny disposition, and rather than becoming cross with her daughter, she glanced toward the carriage glass, caught sight of her hair and joined in the amusement with her own sparkling laughter.

"Shall we cough now?" Hannah asked as they gasped for breath.

Lady Westwich gently cleared her throat and winked at her. "Mary, if you'd be a dear and repair what you can." She waved a hand over the strange construction of her hair.

Mary set to work with magic fingers, smoothing the frizz into pretty waves.

"Now that we've had our fun…" Lady Westwich put her full focus on Hannah in a way that made her chest constrict. "What is this about Lord Brightstone?"

"Whatever do you mean?" Hannah asked innocently.

"A broken fence?" Lady Westwich arched a brow. "A chance encounter? A complete coincidence when we were just saying how you had to find someone to wed?"

Hannah let her head rest back on the cushioned seat behind her. "Please don't do this."

"Does it not seem serendipitous, hmm?" her mother prodded.

"How did you even learn of the broken fence?" Hannah brought her attention from the pink silk top of the carriage to her mother's sly grin.

"I have my ways." Lady Westwich picked at a nonexistent thread on her skirt. "And I didn't tell a soul for a week so your Mary wouldn't learn about it from the staff."

Mary and Hannah glanced at one another, guiltily found out.

"Oh, I've known about Mary's skill at gathering information for years." Her mother waved a hand. "I'm not daft, and I run a tight household." She lifted her chin a notch higher. "I confess, the story I heard about Lord Brightstone was dreadfully boring, and I'd like more details." As she rested her chin on her hand, elbow propped upon her knee, her bright blue eyes met Hannah's. "Do tell."

Hannah sighed and relayed the tale to her mother, knowing she had to be precise with all the details, or Lady Westwich would add concocted suggestions with her own florid detail.

"You do have fine legs." Lady Westwich tilted her head coquettishly when Hannah mentioned her skirts had been tossed up in the fall.

"Mother," Hannah gasped in horror. "That is wildly improper. And anyway, he is a gentleman and averted his gaze."

"He still saw," the baroness whispered loudly to Mary, who grinned in reply.

"The meeting resulted in the saving of a hapless little cat who is now restored with his family in the barn." Hannah held up her hands to demonstrate. "Nothing more."

"Oh, but that all was tremendously romantic, don't you think, Mary?" Lady Westwich raised her brows at Hannah's maid.

"It was, my lady." Mary gave a vigorous nod with the broadest of smiles.

The traitor.

"Well, I would not be surprised to have Lord Brightstone seeking you out soon," Lady Westwich declared.

But Hannah knew the truth. It would be best to put Lord Brightstone from her mind that season—and his pursuit of a wife who was decidedly not Hannah.

WAS THERE anything more torturous than enduring a carriage ride with one's mother when she was set on a marriage match? Lucien gazed at the scenery flickering by in flashes of light from the gas lamps.

"I must say your attire is grand," Lady Brightstone said approvingly, pulling his consideration back to her. "I wager you'll have several women take note of you tonight." She nodded to herself, setting the diamonds at her neck sparkling like frosted ice.

He hoped he did draw some notice to make the discomfort worthwhile. The jacket enveloped him like a second skin against his shoulders and waist, and the breeches were unnaturally snug, particularly across his arse when he sat in the carriage. Admittedly, he did appreciate the deep blue of the waistcoat, noticing for the first time how the color truly did suit him.

Waistcoat aside, he now knew what a sausage felt like in its casing after having never harbored a curiosity for such intimate details of the food's existence.

The carriage rolled to a stop, and Lady Brightstone secured the thick ermine around her shoulders before the door opened. A chill rushed into the small cabin, all the more apparent to Lucien now that he was sporting such close-fitting attire.

He ushered his mother through the grand entrance of Ranford Place into the warm glow of candlelight. After ensuring his mother's fur stole was properly seen to, he escorted her to wait for the caller to announce their entrance into the esteemed first ball of the season.

An unaccustomed bout of nervousness rattled through him. It was vain to anticipate how his new appearance might be received. Or wonder if it might sway people's opinions of him.

He was a bore to others. Their gossip had reached his ears enough times to be well aware of society's perception of him. The realization had not been offensive, however, for the lot of them were equally as uninteresting to him.

And yet, a curious thing happened as he and his mother were announced. Lucien led her into the open ballroom to the rapt interest of nearly every person in attendance. Their focus fell upon him and did not wander away. It lingered. And held.

Women leaned toward one another, their mouths obscured by fans as their gazes locked on his person. Some were going so far as to skim down the expanse of his fitted clothing.

He hoped the burn of his cheeks wasn't as visible to everyone as it felt. For to him, it seemed as though he were a candle lit in the center of a dark room, drawing everyone's eye.

Suddenly, he regretted the damnable clothes, the way the breeches hugged his thighs and the way the tailored jacket nipped in at his waist and hips. He'd once overheard a lady grouse over a man who had a conversation with her bosom rather than her face. Was this how women felt when subjected to men who were untoward?

How did they bloody stand it?

Several women ogled at him as he passed, waiting until the very moment he glanced in their direction before they demurely lowered their heads. What a ridiculous notion when they'd practically bored holes into his skull with their stares. No doubt the lot of them would chuckle at him for being dressed so foppishly.

This had all been a mistake. A foolish, insipid mistake he'd done to please his mother. But now she was happy, and he was even more miserable.

Lady Alison, a woman a year his junior, swept before him.

They had been introduced before. On several occasions, in fact, as she'd always seemed to forget that they were acquainted. Now she let her confident gray gaze take him in before she lowered into a slight curtsey. "Good evening, Lord Brightstone." That audacious stare met his once more. "I trust you are well."

For a moment, he didn't reply. She wasn't mocking him. She wasn't approaching him for sport. And she remembered who he was.

With a flirtatious twist of her shoulders, she batted her eyes at him.

She was…interested.

In him.

"We are both quite well, thank you," his mother replied from beside him after his prolonged silence.

"Indeed," he added daftly.

Lady Alison was not the only woman to approach him. Lady Diana soon followed, a dark-haired beauty with a brilliant smile. Then after her came Miss Smithwick, who gaped up at him.

Truly. A simple haircut and the addition of a few new pieces to his wardrobe—the attention those details garnered was astounding.

A proud smile graced his mother's face as she discreetly nudged him with her hand at his arm, encouraging him deeper into the season's first assembled gathering.

The inhibitions plaguing him upon entry into the ballroom were whisked away, replaced by a strange sense of pride in how others beheld him. He straightened his back a little taller, his shoulders squaring and his smile more ready.

Not that his updated appearance afforded him much in the way of conversation as he bumbled his way through each new woman he spoke with.

"You should be asking every one of these women to dance," Lady Brightstone said under her breath.

He chuckled at the suggestion. "You know I don't dance, Mother."

"After what has been paid on your dance instructors…" She slid him a glare that indicated his reply did not amuse her. "I suggest you learn to enjoy dancing if you intend to acquire a wife." With that, she sailed toward a group of women, freeing him from her oppressive presence.

A pretty brunette near the lemonade smiled at him, and though he returned the gesture, he did not approach. Not when he wasn't sure what to say.

He needed more than simply his attire to be altered. He had to be different in speech and manner as well.

A bright laugh rose suddenly above the orchestra and conversation. He looked toward the sound and his heart caught.

Miss Bexley was in attendance.

Her red hair was styled into an upswept coiffure adorned with pearls and ice-blue ribbons that matched the very shade of her dress, making her eyes stand out like gemstones. A flush of delight warmed her fair cheeks, and the smile on her face was so beatific that his own dampened mood suddenly lightened.

He took a step toward her, drawn in by her vivacity as surely as plants were to the brilliance of the sun, but stopped himself in time. There was no reason to go to her. And if he did, what would he say?

She was surrounded by several other ladies, likely friends of hers.

He would have to interrupt them to speak to her. And with no purpose.

Unless, of course, he sought her counsel on how best to converse with women, the same as he'd previously sought help with his attire. Once she was finished visiting with her friends, of course.

Miss Bexley and the other ladies leaned close and grinned at one another, conspirators in the same shared secret.

Never had he been close acquaintances with others as Miss Bexley and her friends appeared to be.

At least not as an adult. There had been Lord Ranford, whom Lucien had known at school when they were boys, but that had been an age ago. It still afforded Lucien invitations such as the one tonight, but he'd let the bond between them fall away. The earl stood on the other side of the room, engaged in a chat with the Earl of Darington, a man with a wretched reputation.

Lucien wasn't adept at idle chatter per se, but at least it was easier to do so with other men. While he waited for Miss Bexley to complete her conversation in the hope he might catch her alone, he resolved to reconnect with Lord Ranford.

He strode to the other two men and nodded in greeting.

"Sporting a new suit and approaching old friends," Lord Ranford said as he joined them. "Who is this man masquerading as Old Brightstone?"

"Old Brightstone"—the nickname was one he'd acquired back in his school days when the others teased him for being the oldest young man among them, set in his ways and stubborn as anyone's stodgy uncle.

"Perhaps he's trying to put more effort into securing himself a wife," Darington suggested with a flash of his roguish grin. "As we all should." The airy expression on his handsome face suggested he was not at all chagrined at his own lack of effort.

He stood a head taller than Ranford and Lucien, his deep brown eyes nearly black as they scanned the room for his next conquest, his dark hair slightly mussed in a manner women found attractive. Or so Stevens, Lucien's valet, had stated.

Lord Darington was a man who required no improvement on any part of his person to acquire a wife, should he desire to have one. But then, he had always been handsome and charming, knowing exactly what to say at the right time. Even his scandalous behavior was tempered by enough civility and flattery to draw everyone to his side, rather than repelling them.

Lucien, for all his learning and reading, had never been adept at composing the proper reply. At least not promptly. Indeed, he was prone to overthinking to a fault, too careful with his words until the moment slipped by, along with his opportunity to reply. That or, when expediency was necessary, he said precisely the wrong thing.

Darington's gaze settled on one of the women gathered around Miss Bexley, and his eyes lit with interest before a woman in jewel-purple silk flounced into his line of sight. "If you'll excuse me," he muttered. "I'm in need of refreshment."

Lord Ranford shook his head at Darington's abrupt departure. "Are you truly venturing out into the unknown of relinquished bachelorhood?"

Lucien sighed. "I'm being reminded of my duties often."

Ranford gave a slow nod of understanding. "I am being granted a reprieve of guilt for this year after successfully helping Julia debut last season. It shan't last long, so I'll enjoy it as I can. But you..." He gestured to Lucien's attire. "A dashing man such as yourself ought to have your pick of ladies in a room such as this, especially since you've commanded such attention. Every single woman in here is on the hunt to win at the marriage mart."

A laugh emanated from the place in the room where Miss Bexley still spoke with her friends.

Lucien must have turned his attention to them, for Ranford looked in their direction and arched a brow. "Well, at least most of the ladies. That lot seems to have no interest in marriage." A smile curled his lips. "Fascinating lot though they may be."

It did not escape Lucien's notice that Ranford regarded Miss Bexley specifically as he said this.

The women were still huddled together, giggling and whispering, oblivious to every man who strode by, no matter his wealth, name, title or even the cut of his jacket.

It seemed an odd thing for a group of women so beautiful and spirited to be disinclined to wed. Suddenly, he envied the women's ability to choose their role in life.

After all, women could become spinsters. But men of the nobility...the weight of their birthright rested on their shoulders.

There was no denying it—Lucien would *have* to wed.

4

*H*annah was nearly bursting with delight to be in the company of her beloved friends once more. Perhaps it was best they were not near her in Skipton, or she might never return to London. They were the only thing she ever anticipated about the season.

"Someone is looking at you," Elizabeth whispered to her. The periwinkle gown she wore sparkled with beads and made her pale blue gaze stand out against her creamy complexion and chestnut hair. Her gaze slid to the side to demonstrate the direction Hannah should glance.

Hannah's cheeks went hot. There was not merely one someone looking at her, but two.

Lord Ranford, who she had so foolishly lost her head over previously, and Lord Brightstone. The smart cut of his jacket and fitted attire indicated he had taken her advice. As did his shorn hair, no longer falling messy over his brow but carefully combed back and to the side.

Without the distraction of his tresses, his face was hard angles in unexpected ways that were well-suited for him. His high cheekbones and perfect nose complimented his firm mouth. But it was not his hair alone that now revealed his attractive features.

Lord Brightstone cut a fine figure of a man with broad, square shoulders and a narrow waist and hips with calves that didn't need even a hint of padding.

"You're staring." Lucy turned to glimpse behind her, but Hannah grasped her shoulders to still her lest she called even more attention to the gentlemen of their attention.

"It isn't what you think," Hannah gasped.

"Did something happen with Lord Ranford?" Amy asked, her voice soft and maternal.

"No," Jillian replied, her focus going first to Lord Brightstone, then to Hannah in that overly perceptive way she had. "I don't think it was with Lord Ranford."

Hannah set her hands on her hips in exasperation. "How could you possibly know that?" Then she huffed out a sigh. "Very well, it was Lord Brightstone, who has been a neighbor of mine for the entirety of my life, as you well know. And something did happen, but it was too mortifying even to share."

"Did you trip in front of him?" Elizabeth asked sympathetically.

"Did you accidentally walk in on him with one of the servants in the stables?" Lucy's hazel eyes danced with wicked excitement.

"Lucy," Amy admonished.

But Lucy only laughed at the rebuke and splashed a bit of something amber-colored into her lemonade from a flask at her side. Her tight curls had already begun to relax, her glossy dark hair too silky and straight to ever remain curled. No doubt it bothered her maid more than Lucy, who never paid fashion much mind.

"In a manner of speaking, Elizabeth is correct," Hannah said quickly and regaled them with the miserable story. She left out the part about Lord Brightstone seeking her counsel on dress, however. That was not her secret to share.

"Oh, Hannah, that must have been dreadfully embarrassing." Amy put a hand on her arm in a motherly fashion, her warm brown gaze soft in a frame of light blonde ringlets.

"It was." Hannah snapped open her fan, revealing a painting of pink and buttercup yellow roses within, and waved it toward her burning face. "I'm grateful he was so kind about it and had his own man repair the fence, so I didn't have to tell my father."

"That was indeed very kind of him," Amy agreed, a little smile lifted her cherub lips.

Jillian's eyes flashed, and Hannah knew she had an idea. Which was not always a good thing. "You should ask him to dance," Jillian insisted.

"Ladies don't ask men to dance," Elizabeth said, aghast.

Lucy tossed a limp curl over her shoulder. "They should."

"Then you do it." Jillian folded her arms over the bodice of her cranberry velvet gown at the dare, a telltale smile hovering at her lips that suggested she knew very well that Lucy was all bluster with such a threat.

Lucy cast a cursory glance about the room. "Alas, there isn't a man worth the effort here." Her brow lifted as she returned her stare pointedly to Jillian. "Not even the Duke of Dudley."

"The Duke of Dudley?" Elizabeth looked between them. "Why is she staring at you like that, Jillian?"

Jillian's jaw flexed forward with a stubborn resentment they all recognized by now.

"You're about to be betrothed again," Hannah gasped.

"Not if I can help it." Jillian plucked the lemonade from Lucy's hand and took a long sip.

"Hey." Lucy reached for the glass, but Jillian pulled it back from her grasp.

"Do you even have a choice?" Amy's lips clamped down on a frown.

"Am I supposed to?" The bitterness in Jillian's tone suggested she felt otherwise.

Lucy swiped for the lemonade once more. This time, Elizabeth intervened and plucked it from Jillian's gloved hand.

"Lady Elizabeth," a man's voice said from beside Hannah.

Elizabeth spun around in surprise, sloshing liquid from the glass and onto the waistcoat and breeches of Lord Darington, the most eligible bachelor of the season for the last three seasons.

"Oh." Elizabeth tugged a handkerchief from her reticule and dabbed first at his waistcoat, then trailed the spilled liquid down to his breeches. After a series of quick wipes at his crotch, she realized what she was doing and froze in horror.

"Elizabeth," Amy hissed, grabbing her arm back.

Darington grinned, then sniffed the air. "Is that brandy I smell?"

Poor Elizabeth's eyes went wide as dinner plates.

"I have to go to the retiring room." Amy tugged Elizabeth with her. "Will you join me, Lady Elizabeth?"

"Y...yes," Elizabeth stammered as she was tugged away.

Lord Darington regarded Lucy, then Jillian, then Hannah

as the awkwardness of the scene sank in like lead. "I suppose I had best go clean up."

Hannah nodded, rendered mute by the cascade of horrid events.

Lucy's raised brows indicated her shock after his departure. "Did she just touch his..."

"Yes." Jillian cringed, her worried expression following Amy and Elizabeth through the crowd. For as aloof as Jillian could sometimes be, she was very much affected by an inflamed sense of guilt, especially when it came to her friends. "We should check on them."

Suddenly, Lord Ranford was there, standing in front of Hannah. He watched the departing Lord Darington and frowned. "Will you dance with me, Miss Bexley?"

Hannah blinked up at him. Had he seen the exchange? And was now asking her for a dance?

It was on the tip of her tongue to decline when she noted her mother's gaze on her from across the room, bright with rapt eagerness. There would be no escaping from this dance.

Hannah cast an apologetic look to Jillian and Lucy and nodded at Lord Ranford, giving her best attempt to appear delighted with the ill-timed request. "That would be wonderful."

"Lord Darington didn't say anything to upset you, did he?" Lord Ranford asked as he led her toward the dance floor.

Startled, she glanced up at him. His face was a touch too long, yet somehow it paired well with his lean, lanky frame. "Did you mean to protect me from him?" she asked.

Before, she might have been hopeful he would say yes—that he intended to be a hero to rescue her like a knight in one of the romantic books Elizabeth loved to read. Perhaps it was that Lord Ranford had smashed Hannah's heart to pieces previously, but now the thought of him rescuing her was more amusing than appealing.

A blush colored Lord Ranford's face, and he self-consciously smoothed his brown hair back. "You've done so much for my family by helping Julia last season. I would hate for you to be repaid by an errant friend being obnoxious."

"That is most considerate of you, but unnecessary, as he was in no way impolite," Hannah truthfully replied as they took their places across from one another on the dance floor.

Over Lord Ranford's shoulder, Hannah could make out her mother on the other side of the ballroom. Her eyes lit with the over-eager gleam of a mother with a possible future son-in-law locked in her sights.

Hannah suppressed a sigh. "Did Lady Julia enjoy the season last year?" she asked politely.

"So much so, I fear she may force me to endure several seasons before finally selecting a husband." Lord Ranford grinned at Hannah in a way that should have made her heart stutter. She truly had given up hope on him.

Which was for the best.

Their conversation skimmed the surface of polite chatter as it pertained to his sister and the uncommonly frigid temperatures in London before moving on to plans for the following week with who was dining where and when. Even Hannah's mother had stopped craning her neck to spy on them as the song droned on.

At last, their dance came to a blessed end. Hannah scanned the room, hoping for the return of her friends before having to relegate herself to her mother's company.

"Forgive me, Miss Bexley." The masculine voice was soft yet slightly cocky. Strangely familiar.

Hannah's heart apparently recognized Lord Brightstone before her mind could, for her pulse thudded like a rapid drum in her ears.

"Ah, Lord Brightstone." She turned toward him, and her breath caught. He was even more alluring up close with the intensity of his dark blue eyes fixed on her, a muscle clenching at the back of his square jaw.

Yet there was a part of her that missed the shaggy sweep of hair over his brow and the way it had made her fingers ache to brush the waves from his handsome face.

"I didn't realize you were here," she lied.

"Yet I am. Obviously." His mouth stretched into a hard line as he appeared to chastise himself internally for the ridiculous reply.

He looked at Lord Ranford. "Am I interrupting?"

"Not at all. I was just leaving." Lord Ranford bowed to Hannah. "Good evening, Miss Bexley."

Hannah inclined her head to the earl and shifted her attention back to Lord Brightstone. "You do look rather dashing if I may say so."

He ducked his head, the effect sheepish and endearing. "I had wonderful advice from a trusted friend."

Friend.

The word hit its mark at the center of her heart.

Ah, yes, the ever-present reminder of her place in this world.

A friend and nothing more.

She hid the sting of his words behind a smile. "I'm glad to

have given it, especially when my counsel was put to such ideal use."

"Would you care to take a turn about the room with me?" he asked, offering her his arm.

She tilted her head to observe the dancers forming in a line for a Scotch reel on the dance floor. "Would you not care to dance instead?"

"I don't dance." While his smile held a note of apology, the steely determination in his eyes indicated he wasn't sorry enough to change course.

"Don't you?"

"Well, I admit, I don't care to." He lifted his shoulder in a casual shrug. "I prefer not to subject myself or my dance partner to my poor attempts at conversation while on the dance floor."

She nodded as if she understood, though clearly, she didn't. How could anyone not enjoy dancing and conversing?

Dancing was spinning and twirling, and, for one brief moment in a sea of tight-laced civility, it was freedom. Truly, she ought to teach him to be a proper dancer more than alter his attire, but she had been through this waltz of becoming involved with a man who saw her only as a friend before.

It would be best for her heart to abandon the man to his own devices.

"Will you take a turn about the room with me?" He asked again, not letting the matter go.

She ought to decline the invitation and join her friends or even her mother. Except that Lord Brightstone had been so very kind to keep her mishap last month to himself. And so it was that she nodded in agreement and slipped her hand into the warm crook of his arm, which was quite strong and firm beneath her touch.

Not that she ought to notice such things.

The slight scent of him was at once familiar, shaving soap, the aroma of books and that pleasant spice.

Not that she ought to notice such things as how decadent he smelled either.

RELIEF WASHED OVER LUCIEN. For a moment, he had worried Miss Bexley would decline his request, especially when she looked so longingly toward the dance floor.

The hope in her eyes as she regarded the couples lining up for a Scotch reel had him feeling like quite the cad. And perhaps he truly was one.

At the very least, he could have forced himself to endure one dance.

Now, however, she was tucked snuggly against his arm, the citrus notes of her light perfume whispering at the edges of his awareness in a way that made him want a little more.

Perhaps she wished to be dancing with Lord Ranford again. The very thought left a strange sensation tightening in his chest. Seeing the two of them whisk around the dance floor was what had finally broken Lucien's hesitation about approaching her. He wanted her company, her candor and that alluring laugh.

Her gaze skimmed over him now, not with interest, but with the assessment of a tailor. "I truly am impressed with your new attire."

Lively music began to play, filling the ballroom with a well-timed tune.

"I couldn't have done it without your assistance." He spoke louder to be heard over the musicians and led her to the outskirts of the room. It did not escape his notice that several people watched as they ambled by.

"And what do you think of your new look?" she asked. "Do you like it?"

Her question took him aback with the thoughtfulness to consider how he felt. "I confess, it is rather uncomfortable. My looser garments were far more to my taste."

To his surprise, she laughed—that carefree tinkle of joy that seemed to make the entire room glow a bit brighter. A matronly woman nearby frowned in Miss Bexley's direction. The blatant show of disapproval left Lucien with a palpable need to step in front of Miss Bexley protectively.

Especially when Miss Bexley lowered her head, evidently chastened by the woman's rudeness. The display of Miss Bexley's shamed acquiescence to the strict rules of society vexed him. Why must she squelch her delight if it suited her to share it with the world?

But as soon as the thought entered his mind, he knew exactly why. It was the same reason he endured his snugly fitted clothes. The same reason she was in a stiff silk ballgown with bits of itchy lace at the cuff of her puff sleeves and along the neckline of her bodice.

To satisfy the burden of society's rules of which they both must comply.

She looked beautiful, of course, with azure ribbons in her curled hair to match her gown and making her eyes stand out as blue as the deepest ocean. Except that he was acquainted with a different woman, one who stripped off her bonnet at the first opportunity and whose hair was not sculpted coils of glossy copper but wild, fiery waves. There was a freedom to her he had admired greatly when they'd met in the country, and he hated the idea of her carefree nature being tamped down by the heavy bonds of the ton.

"I like your laugh." He said it so abruptly that he rather surprised himself.

Miss Bexley's face turned up toward him, her eyes wide. "I beg your pardon?"

"You have a lovely laugh," he repeated.

Scarlet splotches bloomed over her cheeks and neck. "You don't have to say that."

"Why would I say it if it wasn't true?"

She studied him a moment as though weighing the earnestness of his compliment. "If you are being honest, you truly are the only person in polite company to find my laugh appealing." The corner of her lip tucked down in a self-deprecating smirk. "Ever."

"I suppose I don't entirely know how to operate among polite society," he confessed. "Light conversation, banter, flattery."

When she looked up at him again, she had a pleasant smile. Her mouth had a nice shape, wide with a full lower lip.

Without meaning to, he had created the perfect opportunity to introduce his request that she assist him in learning the subtle nuances of small talk at soirees and ballrooms.

"I see no deficiencies based on our conversation tonight." She spoke softly to ensure their conversation remained private. "There are certain things you can do to keep the discussion flowing. And you can get away with practically anything with a well-timed wink." She winked at him in a demonstration.

"And that is exactly why I wondered if you might consider helping me again."

The corners of her smile seemed to wilt, or perhaps he had imagined it. After all, if she did not wish to aid him, she need only decline. Before he could gauge for certain, she focused on the path of attendees loitering before them.

Lucien steered her around a woman in a ghastly orange dress and painted red lips in an obvious attempt to warrant attention.

"You see, I am somewhat clumsy in the art of light conversation." He winced. "You might have noticed."

"You say what you think," Miss Bexley replied without glancing at him. "I think it's rather admirable."

"Unfortunately, most do not share that opinion."

"I must be honest with you, Lord Brightstone." She stopped and gazed up at him with the force of her stunning blue eyes. "I am hardly the one to instruct you on matters of polite conversation. More times than not, I talk far too much and am not exactly adept at restraining my emotions. What's more, I have failed to attract any suitors of my own. Whatever expertise you may think I possess, you would do well to realize I truly am lacking."

It was her second mention of her inability to attract suitors, an incredulous phenomenon in his eyes.

"How is that?" He stared down at her for a long moment, taking in the flush of her cheeks, the burning conviction in her eyes. How he longed for the stiffness of her hair to be once more unbound and free as it had been when she'd broken his fence in her endeavors to rescue the barn cat.

Perhaps he had been going about this all wrong. Maybe what he needed was directly in front of him the whole time.

Bully to his mother and her unwarranted criticism. At that moment, he knew exactly what he wanted. No, not what. Who.

He wanted Miss Bexley.

She blinked up at him. "Many reasons and truly, none of it matters. I have no plans to wed."

"Don't you?" he asked, even as his conversation with Lord Ranford came back to him.

That lot seems to have no interest in marriage.

Miss Bexley's pointed chin jutted out with stubborn defiance. "I don't. I prefer not to bow to a man's bidding and be subjected to a mother-in-law's displeasure regularly."

Lucien couldn't argue with such a perfectly stated argument. Women were the property of men as surely as any manor house, and if society passed judgment, mothers could be far worse.

Most especially his own.

Still, he could not quell his rising disappointment.

He nodded slowly. "I do understand. However, it is a pity to deprive the members of the ton such vivacity and beauty."

Miss Bexley scoffed. "And you say you need instructions on idle chatter and flattering women."

"I beg your pardon?"

"Sirrah, you are a flirt." She tapped her fan on his forearm, and her gaze lingered on him for a heart-stopping moment.

A flirt?

He frowned. What he had said was simply the truth, not flirtation.

They had nearly finished walking the perimeter of the

ballroom. Their time was almost up, and urgency nudged him to make his request once more. "Would you perhaps please reconsider instructing me on small talk? I tend to be at a loss as to what to say."

Miss Bexley bit that full lower lip and regarded him.

"I genuinely do need help, and you were of such great assistance before," he added with a pleading expression.

She sighed. "Very well, but only because you said you liked my laugh."

"Are you flirting now?" he asked, not entirely certain but well aware how very much he enjoyed it.

In response, she laughed. "I'll be at Almack's on Wednesday. If you care for instruction, be there."

"I will," he promised. "Thank you."

She nodded primly and gave him a small curtsy before departing to join her friends, who had gathered in an intimate circle once more. Suddenly, he was anticipating the season for the first time since he was obliged to attend these droll functions. And that eagerness had everything to do with Miss Bexley.

5

Candles glittered in the elaborate chandeliers overhead. Almack's was filled to the brim with the best the ton had to offer, or so was determined by the Patronesses, who only granted vouchers to the exclusive establishment to those they felt deserving.

Somehow Hannah had managed to stay in their good graces, though heavens, it *did* take effort.

It was nearly eleven o'clock when a light supper—if one could call buttered bread and dry cake supper—would be served, and the doors closed. Except that Lucien had not yet arrived.

Hannah glanced about once more, hating the crush of disappointment in her chest. He had lingered in her mind like a stubborn burr, the spines of their conversation nestled securely against her brain.

He liked her laugh.

No one liked her laugh, least of all her. But he did.

He also thought her vivacious. And beautiful.

Stop.

It was a cycle of thoughts that had churned incessantly since Lord Ranford's ball several days earlier.

"What do you think, Hannah?" Jillian asked.

Hannah blinked and refocused on her friend, realizing she had been asked a question. "Um, yes, I think that would do nicely."

Jillian shared a look with Elizabeth and Amy, and the three giggled delicately behind their fans.

"What is it?" Hannah groaned.

"You, my dear, are distracted," Amy teased gently, pointing a silk-gloved finger at her.

Elizabeth grinned. "Jillian asked what we might do if the room were to rotate suddenly, so the dance floor was on the ceiling."

"Well." Hannah laughed. "I suppose that would *not* do nicely."

"No, indeed," Jillian replied, her lips curling up in a wide smile.

The clock struck eleven.

Amy eyed the clock, setting the small gems in her blonde hair sparkling. "Lucy hasn't made it yet."

"She never makes it," Elizabeth replied. "But do you know who has?" She gazed in the direction of the Duke of Dudley, the man Jillian's father intended for her to wed.

Jillian's head fell back with exasperation. "I do wish my father would leave me be about this marriage business."

"At least he is handsome," Amy said.

It was true. The man had thick, dark hair and a lean frame. What Elizabeth politely omitted was that the man's immensely long nose was often pointed aloft in the air with haughty pride.

"Too bad he knows it," Jillian murmured.

"It could be a romantic match." Elizabeth swept a hand down her pink ballgown, the movement somewhat anxious.

"Now you sound like my mother." Hannah shot Elizabeth an exasperated look. "And why are you so nervous suddenly?"

"Nervous?" Elizabeth squared her shoulders. "I am *not* nervous."

No sooner had she spoken than Lord Darington walked by with his dark gaze locked on her. The delicate muscles in Elizabeth's neck stood out, and she swallowed hard.

"Lord Darington, truly?" Hannah whispered.

But then, Lord Brightstone crossed the room as the crowd began to move into the supper rooms. Heat sizzled in her veins.

"Lord Brightstone," Elizabeth whispered back. "Truly?"

Hannah nudged her friend with her elbow good-naturedly, and Elizabeth laughed. Both women had been caught eyeing men of interest.

"He seems very sweet," Amy chimed in, evidently having overheard.

"Lord Darington?" Hannah asked with an innocent air.

The four of them laughed once more.

"A man that sinful would be better with the likes of Lucy." Jillian tossed her hair over her shoulder, having only half the mass of dark waves bound up. It wasn't in style, but Jillian was never one to conform to fashion.

"Even Lord Darington wouldn't know what to do with Lucy," Hannah retorted and they all giggled once more.

Amy led them toward the supper rooms, the green brocade gown she wore brushing the floor as she did so. "I meant Lord Brightstone."

Hannah scrunched her face, wishing they would let the topic drop.

Jillian glanced toward the earl of their discussion, and her expression became pensive in a way that made Hannah's nerves fray. Her friend always saw far too much.

"Oh, look, tea and cake," Hannah said as they entered the room.

"They always have tea and cake," Elizabeth retorted dryly. "I think you're trying to change the subject."

They each took a thinly sliced piece of buttered bread, and Hannah bit into her snack to fill her mouth before having to answer.

She didn't want her friends to encourage her toward Lord Brightstone. Keeping her heart guarded around him was already difficult enough without their cajoling and prodding. Without them trying to instill false hopes in a place that ought not to foster any.

They meant well, of course. However, after the pain of Lord Ranford's disinterest, Hannah could not stand the idea of suffering through another failed romance.

No, it was better for things to remain strictly instructional with Lord Brightstone.

By some strange pull of fate, she glanced about the room and caught sight of the earl standing only three people away from her. The beat of her heart snagged.

He was even more handsome up close. Even more than several nights ago at Lord Ranford's ball. His blue eyes found hers, and a thrill tingled through her.

"Hannah, are you well?" Amy's hand on her arm recalled Hannah back to her friends.

"Oh, yes." She shook her head at herself. "I'm simply

marveling at how thin this bread is. Really, it's fascinating, don't you think? It can scarce hold the spread of butter over it."

Elizabeth's brows pinched, and her mouth opened in a partial question, confirming that Hannah's behavior was… well…strange.

She shoved a bit of food in her mouth to silence her frenzied chatter.

"Hannah is not well," Jillian murmured.

Hannah smiled around her bite of bread and shrugged. The swallow that followed, however, was unsuccessful going down as the dry lump lodged itself in her throat.

"Here, let me help." Elizabeth fetched a cup of lemonade and handed it to Hannah.

Thankfully, the tart, watered-down drink was enough to force the clump of bread down Hannah's throat.

"Goodness, that could have been dreadful." She smiled gratefully at Elizabeth. "I don't understand why they make the bread thin if it's to be so very dry. Surely, I'm not the only one who has choked on it." She chuckled in a self-deprecating form, even as she internally chastised herself for the idle, anxious chatter. "At least there is some cake to be had. I could—"

An icy glare from Lady Arksford halted Hannah's nervous babble. The older woman was a close acquaintance of one of the patronesses of Almack's and might well be holding Hannah's voucher to the coveted establishment to a proverbial flame.

It wasn't the first time Lady Arksford had been offended by Hannah. At least this time, the older woman hadn't publicly reprimanded her as had been done last season at a dinner party. The countess's rebuke for Hannah to be quiet had been sharp as a whistle, cutting through the busy room so that everyone stopped speaking for the briefest of moments to look at Hannah.

Even now, her body burned with mortification at the memory, and she went silent at once.

"Don't mind her," Jillian said fiercely in Hannah's ear. "People are afraid of those who are different from them."

No one knew the truth behind those words better than Jillian, who was as unique a person as they came. It was one of the many things they all adored about her.

Hannah grasped her friend's hand in gratitude.

"Oh," Elizabeth moaned miserably.

The buttered side of the bread had tumbled onto her lovely pink gown, leaving a greasy splotch on the fine carnation-colored silk of her bodice.

A handkerchief appeared out of nowhere, held out by a gentleman in a fine, perfectly fitted suit with neatly combed blond hair.

Hannah's heart nearly tumbled out of her chest.

Lord Brightstone.

Though his hand was extended to Elizabeth, it was Hannah's gaze he held. "Miss Bexley." His jaw was freshly shaven and smooth and his waistcoat was a deep navy that was agreeable with the blue of his eyes.

"Oh, Lord Brightstone, I'm so pleased you could make it." The tension strung over Hannah's nerves jittered suddenly to life until it seemed as though her insides were vibrating. "I noticed you hadn't arrived at half-past ten and worried." Horror descended upon her like a splash of ice water as she realized she'd confessed to noticing his comings and goings. "I mean to say that I expected you and didn't happen to see you about…" she stammered.

Amy gently cleared her throat, bringing the embarrassing gush of words to a halt as Hannah realized she had yet to introduce the earl to her friends.

"Forgive me. Ladies, this is the Earl of Brightstone." Hannah indicated Jillian first. "This is Lady Jillian." Next, she motioned to Elizabeth, then Amy. "And Lady Elizabeth and Miss Honeyfield. We usually have Miss Lucy Beauchamp in attendance with us as well."

"She was unable to make it," Lady Jillian supplied with a graceful curtsey.

Lady Elizabeth paused mid-wipe at her butter-smeared bodice and smiled shyly. Whatever her efforts were, they were in vain. The stain of grease seemed to be spreading rather than wiping away.

Lord Brightstone bowed regally to Hannah's friends. "Well met." To Hannah, he said, "Shall we take a turn about the room?"

"Perhaps a dance would be in order." Jillian's suggestion was softly given but loud enough to have been heard by all of them.

Unfortunately.

Hannah speared her friend with a hard, pointed look.

"Lord Brightstone doesn't care to dance," Hannah supplied.

"No," Lord Brightstone said thoughtfully. "But perhaps now would be a decent time to refresh myself."

Startled, Hannah blinked up at him.

He winked at her.

Blast him for being such a quick study.

He offered her his arm as people began to relocate to the ballroom. She accepted and slid her cold hand into the heat at the crook of his elbow. He was warm and strong, and she hated how much she wished she could relish that moment.

After all, she was only an instructor. Her role was a reminder she would do best to keep in the forefront.

He led her to the dance floor, and every female eye in the room followed them. They gazed upon Lord Brightstone with open interest and anticipation. And they watched her with a fiery hatred.

Little did they know she was no threat at all. She never was, and never would be, competition for any woman.

Lucien assumed his place in front of her. Too late, she realized exactly what they would be dancing, even as the opening cords strummed to life.

Of course, it had to be the waltz.

IT HAD BEEN an age since Lucien had danced. Truly, the act was one he did not relish. How he hated being put in a situation to have to drum up idle conversation for the amusement of one's companion regardless of his lack of interest.

But then, he had never danced with Miss Bexley before.

He hadn't realized the set would be the waltz when he'd led her to the dance floor but was grateful for it now. She looked lovely this evening in a violet silk gown with amethysts glittering from her slender throat. Her waist appeared impossibly slender and begged him to span it with his hands. Now would at least present an opportunity to hold her, to stare into the blue of her lovely eyes and speak more intimately than if they were taking a turn about the room.

She moved with a delicate grace, something he'd immediately noticed when she'd drifted across the floor with Lord Ranford.

Now she would be dancing with Lucien. An edge of pride inched his spine a little taller. From the side of the ballroom, Miss Bexley's friends watched them.

Suddenly, he realized she likely had told them of his request for her help. While he shouldn't care if her friends knew, there was a part of him that was embarrassed for others to know or should see him as pathetically as he'd revealed himself to be to Miss Bexley. It was ridiculous, of course. Why should he care what they thought of him when he was so open with discussing the matter with Miss Bexley?

"You needn't worry about my telling them," she replied under her breath as they stepped together and clasped hands overhead. "It is your secret to keep or share."

"Was my concern so obvious?" He smiled in quiet thanks as he slipped his hand around her narrow waist. The fabric of her gown was cool and slick against his palms. It made him long to stroke his touch up her back to her skin to see if it was even smoother still.

"A little." She winked, and her hand went to his waist as well, bringing them so close together that he could see every freckle that dusted the bridge of her pert nose.

That sweet, clean scent of her swept into his awareness and had him longing to be nearer still.

"I know I have a propensity to talk too much." She gazed up at him as she spoke in a way that left him feeling like the only man in the entire world.

"I don't mind it."

She glanced away slightly as he began to guide them in a careful spin about the room. On either side of them, the world whirled by in a blur so that she was his only constant, his only focus that did not move.

"You dance very well." She said it as though this was a shock to her.

"I told you I can dance, but that I don't care to."

She rolled her eyes playfully. "And here I wore my most robust slippers in the anticipation that you'd be stomping on my feet all night."

He glanced down at the black silk slippers that appeared anything but sturdy, careful not to upset their balance as their turning ceased. "I dare say those are about as appropriate for a night of accosted toes as those house slippers were for climbing fences."

She laughed aloud. "Admittedly, I shouldn't have been climbing your fence to begin with."

"And leave Leaf to suffer his own devices?" He grinned.

The expression she gave him was one of faux admonishment. "You know I couldn't."

It was his turn to chuckle. "And how is the furry chap?"

They repositioned their hands on one another as the tune subtly shifted, so her delicate touch was on his shoulders. Together, they deftly twirled around the center ballroom, her footsteps light and graceful over the glossy wood floor. Each shift of her body was discernible beneath her gown and his gloves, granting him a sensual tease he had not been expecting.

"Leaf is a barn cat through and through," Miss Bexley replied with a huff of exasperation. "I tried to have him sleep in my room after he nearly tumbled to his death, and he cried all night at the window. Wild little beast. I kept him there until his paw was fully recovered, but he wasn't at all grateful for the disruption to his life."

Lucien could imagine Miss Bexley and the stubborn creature as she tried to cajole and heal the cat. He couldn't help but laugh out loud.

"It isn't all that funny," she said with a smile blossoming on her face. "Or perhaps it is."

A comfortable silence fell between them as they stared into one another's eyes. The music altered once more, and they walked side by side, a brief respite to catch their breath.

"So, tell me, Lord Brightstone." Miss Bexley watched him imploringly. "How could you possibly feel you are deficient in conversing with ladies?"

He lifted his shoulder. "I never know what to say."

"There haven't been any delays or uncomfortable pauses in our discussion. I confess I've been enjoying our banter."

Banter?

Ah, yes, the playful back and forth that seemed so easy between them. He had never engaged in banter with anyone else before. At least, not that he could recall.

It was rather amusing. Something he would not mind indulging in again in the future.

"It's easy with you," he replied. "Because you're..."

He almost said charming but stopped himself at the last moment, uncertain if she would presume that he was attempting to flatter her, to woo her. If he needed her help, it would not do to have her suspect he wanted more than the friendship they had established.

"Kind?" she replied.

"I beg your pardon?" he asked as he took her hand overhead once more, twirling her to the lively tune.

"Talking is easy with me because I'm kind," she supplied. "Is that what you meant to say?"

"Yes, of course." He smiled at her, but strangely she didn't return the gesture. Instead, she glanced away, and the easiness between them crumbled.

Clearly, he had said something wrong.

"When you speak with a woman while dancing," she said in a measured, thoughtful tone, "the polite topics are the weather, fashion and non-political events about London, but not gossip."

"And if they gossip?" he asked dryly. Because the ladies with whom he had endured dances with previously always gossiped.

Always.

She grimaced and shrugged as they came to a stop. "Endure it for civility's sake?"

He sighed, and she chuckled. "It's not all that bad," she scolded.

He arched an eyebrow at her mirth. "So you say."

"Come, I'll pretend to be a lady you're interested in." Miss Bexley squared her shoulders as they clung to one another and spun in the dizzying waltz. After clearing her throat, she gave him a doe-eyed stare, her lips poised in a caricature of a smile. "Lord Brightstone, how good of you to ask me to dance." Her voice rose and fell with great inflection, like an overdramatized actress.

A snort sounded in the back of his throat.

"I'll pretend not to be offended by that," she supplied haughtily.

"How magnanimous." He grinned and stopped their whirling, putting his hand to her lower back once more and walking side by side with her as the dance slowed. "I say, what do you think of the weather today?"

"It's been windy and rather cold." She tilted her shoulder, continuing the snobbish drawl. "Fortunately, I have several furs with which to bury beneath at home while reading such literary works as *Pride and Prejudice*."

"*Pride and Prejudice*?" He nearly missed a step in the dance.

"Of course," she said in her normal voice, once more Miss Bexley. "The story is divine. Elizabeth went on about it at such lengths, we all ended up reading—and adoring—the book. Have you read it?"

He hesitated, halting his knee-jerk response before it could rush from his mouth.

She leaned away from him. "You're baring your teeth at me."

He closed his lips, not realizing he'd held them open. "I am not."

"You are," she accused with a laugh. "Tell me what you mean to say."

"Frankly, I wouldn't waste my time with such drivel," he replied, grateful to have been given leave to break the dam of his thoughts. "Not when there are better works to engage my time."

She narrowed her eyes at him, and he kicked himself for that response, knowing it would likely earn him a rebuke.

"Well, it must be noted, that is not how to respond when dancing with a lady," she chided lightly.

The music slowed, and the dance came to an end. He bowed.

She curtseyed, but as she rose, she said, "Have you read the book at all, or are you judging it simply on the audience to whom it appeals?"

To that, he did not have a response. At least not one he cared to voice.

Miss Bexley lifted her brow, her point made. "In that case, I have many books to recommend, but I would suggest you start with *Pride and Prejudice*." Her lips teased upward. "It may be enlightening."

Despite himself, he grinned. There was an openness about Miss Bexley that appealed to him greatly. She said exactly what was on her mind without preamble or prevarication.

"And you ought to dance more." She slid her hand into the crook of his proffered arm. "You're quite good."

He should be after the countless years of instruction he had been subjected to. For now, he was grateful it afforded him such a delightful time with Miss Bexley.

"So, in summary: dance with ladies, keep conversation to the weather and fashion and endure gossip when it's presented," he said, organizing her advice into a succinct statement. "And read *Pride and Prejudice*."

She smiled. "When next I see you, I wager I will be toasting to your success as the most eligible bachelor of the season."

It was such a preposterous concept when he had been thus far invisible all these years. He nearly scoffed. He was certainly not the sort to attract much attention, but he could at least perform the small suggestions she had given him. Even reading *Pride and Prejudice*.

The following day after breakfast, a small parcel was delivered to him with his name written on the back of an envelope in a beautiful slanted script. The small card within was filled with the same elegant handwriting.

To ensure you don't forget to read it. Enjoy!

Thoughtfully,

Miss Bexley

He knew what the item was before he even peeled back the paper wrapper and was not at all surprised that she had gifted him with his very own copy of the first volume of *Pride and Prejudice*.

6

Hannah almost leapt from her seat every time their butler entered the drawing room where she was painting a watercolor of their garden. Or at least what their garden looked like when it wasn't stripped bare by winter's wrath.

Surely Lord Brightstone would have received her gift by now. And surely etiquette would dictate that he replied with thanks.

But then, he didn't seem to always abide by all the points of etiquette, which was one of the many things she liked about him. He was perhaps one of the few people in her life that did not make her feel as if she had to be perfect.

Thus far, no note had arrived, and she tried hard not to be disappointed. After all, he had requested her instruction to attract a wife. One who was decidedly not her. He owed her no correspondence.

"Oh, Hannah." Lady Westwich clasped her hands over her heart. "You are such a divine artist!"

Her mother rushed over to examine the almost completed

painting. It was nothing special, merely a way of passing the time with a few strokes here and there with the paintbrush. Hannah's talent was, at best, average by her objective consideration. Indeed, it was nothing like Jillian's skill, who could create a piece twice as good in half the time.

"When this is complete, I should like it to be framed for my room," Lady Westwich declared.

"You already have several on display," Hannah replied. "Most of them are far better than this."

Her mother tsked. "Every one you do is a stunning piece of art. Don't you ever tell yourself anything different." She embraced Hannah between brush strokes. "Truly, you are so talented."

At that moment, Lord Westwich entered the drawing room with a newspaper folded in his hands.

"Henry," her mother called, waving him over. "Do come look at this beautiful painting our Hannah has created."

His face immediately lit up, and he approached the window. "Hannah, you've outdone yourself on this one." He settled a hand on her shoulder and squeezed it gently, his eyes crinkling at the corners with affection and love.

It made her wish she could be the person her parents thought she was.

"Your mother will likely want that one for her bedchamber." He removed his hand from Hannah's shoulder and smiled at his wife, leaving Hannah grateful for the redirection of his attention from her.

"That's precisely what I told her," Lady Westwich said proudly. "And since you are here, I believe we were going to discuss the invitations for our dinner party next week."

Her father's dark brows lifted. "Oh. Yes. The dinner party

invitations, of course." He nodded so enthusiastically that Hannah immediately suspected the gears of a plot were turning.

Lord Westwich was always a willing player in her mother's schemes. Only, he was a terrible actor.

"Who are you planning to invite?" Hannah asked innocently, even as dread curdled in her stomach.

"Oh, the usual," her mother began. "Most likely Lord and Lady Whimbly as well as Lord and Lady Hasselton."

Which left an open spot for a single gentleman to be included. How very transparent. Hannah squelched an enormous sigh.

"Ah, but we cannot have our seats so uneven, my love," Lord Westwich said in an unnatural tone, as though reading from a card.

"Is it uneven?" The baroness gasped and put her hand over her mouth.

Hers was a far stronger performance than that of Lord Westwich. Hannah would give her mother that.

"How careless of me," Lady Westwich continued. "Perhaps…perhaps our Hannah might have a suggestion?"

"Yes, Hannah," her father said woodenly. "Can you think of someone who might help us even out the guests?"

Hannah curled the damp tip of her brush around a rose petal, bleeding carnation pink onto the paper. "Hmmm…I can't possibly imagine who we could invite. Perhaps Lord Ecklesby?"

The irascible old baron had never wed, instead devoting his life to hatred and invectives. If nothing else, he would be entertaining. And even his unpleasant personality would be preferable to having—

"Lord Brightstone," her mother exclaimed as though she had not even heard Hannah's reply. "What a wonderful suggestion."

"I didn't say Lord Brightstone," Hannah protested.

Her father looked at her, partly with curiosity, partly with horror at being in a position where Hannah had not answered as he had been instructed she would. He swallowed. "Eh…yes, I think Lord Brightstone will be the perfect addition." His expression softened, and his voice returned to normal. "If that's what you truly want, Hannah."

Lady Westwich folded her arms over her chest and shot a glare at her husband.

Hannah sighed in resignation. In truth, it would be better to have Lord Brightstone in attendance so she could tutor him more in casual dinner conversation. Because really, that would be the only reason for him to attend.

Not that he genuinely needed assistance in how to speak with women when he'd been so very charming with her at Almack's. Her pulse kicked up at the recollection of his strong hands about her waist, his face so close that she could discern small flecks of green near his irises and a light scar near his hairline over his left brow.

He had intrigued her and made her laugh, something she felt comfortable doing after he had told her he liked the sound of it. She still did not believe he didn't mind that she talked so much. However, if he truly did not, he would be the only man to say so, aside from her father.

A memory flitted back to her from her debut ball when having emerged from the retiring room, she had happened upon two men she'd danced with earlier that evening—a dashing earl and a handsome viscount. Neither saw her standing there in the shadows, but both lamented at having to suffer through her talking nonstop through the course of the dance.

Sheer torture, one had called it, as the other laughed and nodded in agreement.

Heat suffused her face even now to recall that horrible moment. After that, she had tried desperately to squelch her laughter and her chatter. The attempt had lasted only a day when the suffocating force of her own self-imposed rules became too much to bear, and she practically exploded to Mary over everything that had happened.

Hannah had never tried again. There was no point in denying who she was when her personality was too strong, even for her own will to suppress.

"I think it will be fine to have Lord Brightstone," Hannah finally replied.

The tension in her father's shoulders relaxed, though his gaze remained somewhat concerned. Hannah schooled her features to keep him from detecting any reservations she held. And there were many.

"Wonderful." Lady Westwich clapped her hands. "I'll see to the invitations straight away."

The butler entered the room with a salver held aloft in his right hand. "A letter has arrived for you, Miss Bexley." Jones extended the tray toward her, and the brilliant afternoon light reflected off the polished silver.

Hannah lifted the letter, unable to quell the moment of breathless anticipation that suddenly seized her.

Miss Bexley,

Thank you for your generous gift. I avow to put it to good use.

With sincerity,

Brightstone

Brightstone. His signature was less formal than Lord Brightstone or the Earl of Brightstone. But nor was it so intimate as to reveal his Christian name.

His reply was easy and smooth, far more so than the letter she had spent the better part of the night composing once she'd returned from the ball. Her rubbish bin had been overflowing with balled-up bits of paper, some too prim, some too florid and others too flowery.

"Who has written to you and left you with such a smile on your face?" Her mother peered at the letter.

Hannah tried to pull it from Lady Westwich's view, but the baroness was too quick in her eagerness.

"Lord Brightstone," she crowed after having read the neatly slanted name.

Hannah folded the note to place in her pocket in time to see the victory cross her mother's features as she nodded to her husband with a smugness that said, "I told you so."

"Do excuse me." Hannah slipped the painting apron off. "I must prepare my gown for Lord and Lady Langston's ball."

"Yes, yes," her mother said distractedly as she no doubt envisioned a future with an elaborate wedding at St. George's Church followed by at least a dozen grandchildren.

But Hannah knew there would be no wedding, and it was better that way.

The ball tonight was to be at Elizabeth's parents' home at Langston Place, and Lord Brightstone would be in attendance. Hannah anticipated the event with equal parts excitement and dread.

She recalled how the ladies watched the earl now that his fine figure was apparent in his immaculately tailored clothing, and more than one eligible debutante had watched him sweep Hannah through the waltz with hungry anticipation in her eyes.

He would be popular at the ball, which was exactly what he wanted. And exactly what she wanted.

Why then did it feel as though a stone was lodged where her heart ought to be?

THE BALLROOM at Langston Place was filled with revelers in a resplendent array of heavy velvets to ward away the brutal winter chill that seemed to grow colder as the evening progressed. Lucien barely felt winter's icy reach as he led his mother into the ballroom, scanning the surrounding faces to determine if Miss Bexley was already in attendance. As her friend's parents were hosting the ball, he anticipated she would have arrived early.

"I trust you will have no difficulty engaging ladies to speak with this evening," his mother said as he guided her toward a cluster of her stuffy friends.

"Why do you say that?" he absently asked as he located Lady Elizabeth and Lady Jillian and continued to seek out a head of glossy red hair near the women.

"Because every lady in the room is staring at you, my son," Lady Brightstone replied.

He took in the bold gazes of several women, who demurely lowered their eyes when he met them. Yes, many women were openly watching him, silently staking their interest.

The banter he'd engaged in with Miss Bexley during their

dance had been enjoyable. He hoped it would be as much so with other ladies of the ton. Maybe he had been wrong about his marriage fears this whole time.

Perhaps it could truly be something pleasant.

He escorted his mother to Lady Arksford, her dearest friend, and left the two whispering frantically to one another as he pretended that their quiet words weren't about him. That was when he saw her—Miss Bexley with her fiery hair piled in curls atop her head and bound with a length of emerald-green ribbon. She wore a matching frock that made her skin glow like fresh cream.

A dance with her first would be best. To obtain several last-minute tips on how best to speak and behave. And, of course, to thank her for the book.

Doubtless, the missive he penned was inadequate. He'd written it several dozen times, foolishly nervous as he weighed each word. It had taken the better part of an hour to decide how best to sign it.

First, he'd gone with Lucien, but that was too familiar. Yet, Lord Brightstone had seemed so overly formal.

Now he couldn't recall exactly what he'd written, only that it had seemed sufficient.

"Lord Brightstone." A lady in a bright pink gown and stiff blonde curls stepped into his path.

He politely smiled as he focused behind her to keep an eye on where he'd seen Miss Bexley.

"Lady Alison." She batted her lashes, and he briefly wondered if she had something in her eye. "Do you recall?"

How ironic that she now worried if he recalled her even as she had always forgotten him in the past.

"Ah, yes." He nodded with an aloof air. "So good to see

you." He shifted slightly and turned his attention from her, ready to stride toward Miss Bexley.

"I thought the same when I discovered you were also in attendance." She blinked up at him, her gray eyes imploring. "My dance card isn't full...yet."

Every morsel of his being begged to be away from the woman's heavy presence. And yet, he was not there to dance solely with Miss Bexley. He was attending all those awful social events with a mind toward marriage. And Lady Alison was definitely interested.

"Would you care to dance with me later this evening?" he asked.

"We can dance now." She bounced a little higher on her toes. Her curls did not move with the action, but her generous bosom jiggled.

Lucien purposefully averted his gaze. "Forgive me, but I have already promised the first set to another."

Lady Alison gave him a pout that immediately told him he would not enjoy life with her and already regretted the solitary dance he would be forced to endure.

"The next one then?" she pressed.

"It would be an honor," he said, though he genuinely wanted to reply with "If I must."

Finally, she left him, freeing him to go to Miss Bexley.

At least until a woman walked headlong into him, sending her fan plopping to the ground at his feet. He hurriedly bent to pick it up for her.

The young woman had dark hair, green eyes and far too much rouge. She giggled as he handed her the fan. "Thank you. How very clumsy of me." She giggled again, and he realized their collision had not been accidental at all.

How very vexing.

"Think nothing of it." He smiled tightly.

"Lord Brightstone, do you truly not remember me?" she asked in a lightly chiding tone.

He did not.

"Miss Closewell. From Yorkshire." She lifted her brows and waited for recognition to dawn.

It did not.

Yorkshire as a hint did nothing to aid in his mental catalog, as he was unsure if she meant they had met there or if her father had an estate there. Either way, the entire conversation felt as much a ruse as their bumping into one another.

What was this world coming to with ladies feigning introductions having been made for an opportunity to speak to a bachelor at a ball?

"It is good to see you again, Miss Closewell," he replied through gritted teeth.

"I hear the orchestra they've hired tonight is supposed to be the best in London." She beamed up at him.

Yet another ploy to get him to ask her to dance. Except that he had about enough of this.

"Indeed," he muttered. "Do excuse me."

With that, he brushed past her and made his way to Miss Bexley in haste, a man on a mission, albeit somewhat haunted by Miss Closewell's powerful rose perfume.

As he approached, Lady Elizabeth turned abruptly from the group and ran headlong into him in a true accident that sent her forehead directly into his nose. Pain exploded through his face and left his eyes watering.

"Oh heavens, I didn't even see you there." Lady Elizabeth gasped. "I'm so very sorry."

He wriggled his nose, hoping the warmth he felt was not blood but too polite to brush his glove against a nostril to confirm. "Please don't trouble yourself over it."

"Lord Brightstone." Miss Bexley rushed to his side and set her long, graceful fingers at his forearm. "Are you hurt?"

Of course, he was bloody well hurt, when the force of someone's head had slammed into one of the more sensitive parts of the human body. But the concern in Miss Bexley's eyes was the greatest balm there was, and he found himself smiling like a simpleton as he shook his head.

"Too bad it wasn't Dudley you ran into," Lady Jillian jested, setting the rest of the ladies—including the shame-faced Lady Elizabeth—smiling at the thought.

Whoever Dudley was, Lucien did not envy the man.

He sniffed heartily and wriggled his nose again. "I wished to see if Miss Bexley would be good enough to spare me a dance."

"You seemed quite popular when you first entered into the ballroom," she replied, a wariness to her tone that did not sit well with him. "Are you certain you wish to spend your first dance with me?"

"Hannah," Miss Honeyfield hissed in her direction.

Miss Bexley colored.

"There's no one I'd rather dance with first at this ball than you," he replied.

She nodded and took his arm. "Are you certain you aren't hurt?" she whispered as he led her to the dance floor.

"No," he said honestly. "It hurt like the very devil, but poor Lady Elizabeth appeared as though she wanted to melt into the floor. Be honest with me now. Am I bleeding?"

Miss Bexley turned her gaze up toward his nose with a

furrow of empathy knitting her brows. "No, there is no blood."

"Thank God for small mercies." Lucien sniffed once more.

"It was kind of you to spare her feelings," Miss Bexley said softly. "She's rather sensitive." There was a tender glint in her eye as she spoke, but she blinked it away and redirected her attention to him. "Now, tell me what I can do for you. I'm assuming there's a reason you asked me to dance."

Because he couldn't stop thinking about her. Because he wanted to breathe in the heady scent of her sweet citrus perfume. Because he loved the carefree tinkle of her laugh and the way he could say whatever popped into his mind without fearing her judgment.

Because he was a damn fool.

"I thought you might give me a few more pointers before sending me out into the wild this evening," he said instead.

"Do you liken ladies of the ton to denizens of the wilderness?" she asked with mirth dancing in her sea-blue eyes.

Lucien recalled the women who had thrown themselves in his path when he tried to make his way to Miss Bexley and tilted his head in gentle acquiescence. This made her laugh as they arrived at the dance floor and took their positions from one another.

It was a quadrille this time, though Lucien would have much preferred for it to be the waltz again. In this dance, they would be separated often, sharing each other with the couple they danced across from.

Their conversation continued in snatches and quick, one-word replies as they danced from one partner to another before finally ending up together once more. Yet somehow, it wasn't maddening but enjoyable. Each separation made him all the more eager for her return to hear what she truly did think of the puffed sleeves that were newly into fashion and exactly how large might be *too* large.

When the dance finally ended, his cheeks ached from smiling.

"You've nothing to fear, Lord Brightstone," she said, her face aglow. "Your conversation leaves nothing wanting, I assure you. Remember, when all else fails, ask questions that will keep them talking. It will always prevent moments of silence from stretching out too long."

He nodded at the final piece of advice and delivered her to her friends. However, as he made good on his promise to dance with Lady Alison, he dreaded the prospect of having to engage in banter with another lady.

If only Miss Bexley could be his dance partner for the whole of the evening.

And if only she truly did wish to wed.

7

Perhaps it was the shrimp.

Hannah's stomach clenched with unease. Her fingers gripped the lemonade cup hard enough to crack the delicate glass.

Lucy sidled up to her, then innocently looked about as her fingers moved in her reticule. "You appear to need this more than me," she whispered and dumped the contents of her flask into Hannah's lemonade.

Hannah shrugged and sipped the drink. There was a neat burn at the end that slid through her, loosening knots of tension as it went down.

Perhaps it was not the shrimp.

Lord Brightstone swept past on the dance floor with Lady Alison, whose girlish giggle followed them, echoing in Hannah's brain. The unease in her stomach coiled tighter once more.

Perhaps it was *him*.

"Lady Jillian." The Duke of Dudley joined their small

group and bowed. "I should like you to do me the honor of a dance."

Jillian turned easily to him, a smile plastered on her lips. "Can you imagine if the room was filled with water, and we were dancing beneath the surface instead? Our ribbons curling up to the surface like resplendent seaweed, our hair shimmering about us like mermaids."

"But we are not underwater," the Duke of Dudley replied dryly.

"Well, that isn't nearly as fun," Jillian sighed.

The duke held out his hand to her as she hesitated for the blink of a second before accepting the unwelcome offer. He took her hand, and together they sailed off toward the dance floor and a fate she'd never wanted.

"Do excuse me," Elizabeth said. "My mother wishes to speak with me. I'll return in a moment."

She drifted away, leaving Lucy and Hannah alone, as Amy had been taken to the dance floor earlier by Lord Ranford.

"He's becoming quite popular, your Lord Brightstone." Lucy watched the dance floor, her hazel eyes locked on the earl as he swirled Lady Alison around the room. Again.

Of all the women in attendance, Lady Alison was hardly the one she expected Lord Brightstone to dance with a second time. No doubt the other woman bullied her way into that extra dance. It was, after all, her way.

"He isn't *my* Lord Brightstone," Hannah hissed.

From across the room, Lady Brightstone glared at her in a manner that was entirely unwelcoming. A chill squeezed Hannah's spine.

"It's as though he suddenly knows exactly what to wear

and say," Lucy continued. "Do you think that is somewhat strange?"

"Hmm?" Hannah turned to her friend. "How so?"

"It's almost as if someone has been instructing him on fashion," Lucy mused.

Hannah took an unladylike gulp of the spiked lemonade, then fought to squelch the cough as the powerful alcohol hit the back of her throat like fire. "I don't even know what you mean," she croaked.

Lucy said nothing and simply lifted a brow. "Do you remember Lady Alison from when we were all at Lady Finch's?"

Hannah groaned and rolled her eyes. "How could we forget when she made it known to everyone that her father was once honored by the king, and we had to kiss the ground she walked upon?"

Lucy snorted. "Remember when you happened upon her in a compromising position with the stable hand?"

Hannah giggled. "I'd never seen a man's chest before then."

"You saw a lot more than that." Lucy laughed and shook her head. "I can't believe you never told anyone."

"It was none of my business," Hannah replied nonchalantly. Seeing Lady Alison chuckle at something Lord Brightstone said made Hannah wish she could go back in time and ruin the spoiled young woman.

The vehemence of her thought startled Hannah. She wasn't an unkind person. What was causing this awfulness to well up inside her and make her consider such ugly sentiments?

A tightness squeezed at her chest that left her feeling as though she couldn't breathe around it.

The music finally stopped, and the dance ended. But as Lord Brightstone escorted Lady Alison off the dance floor, a small crowd of women gathered around him, all fluttering lashes and overeager grins.

All at once, the swirl of people became too pressing, the heat from the candles overhead and the hearth fires were so hot, perspiration prickled at her brow, and the air was thick and sluggish in her chest. She shoved her lemonade into Lucy's hand and fled the room, desperate for a chance to breathe again, to clear her head and heart.

She shoved out the door to the terrace, where an icy February breeze enveloped her overheated body like a breath of fresh air. No one else was outside, and why would they be? Only someone mad would be on the terrace in the middle of the most frigid winter in London.

The air burned her lungs as she inhaled, but the fog in her mind began to lift finally. She had allowed herself to get too involved with Lord Brightstone. And blast it all, she knew better.

There had been too many times where she had done this before. Men were drawn to her because she was kind to them, and she genuinely did want to help them. But then, as time went on, her heart became invested.

And theirs did not.

How many times would she do this to herself? How many times would she lose herself with a man when she knew her lack of appeal as a potential wife?

The door to the ballroom opened.

"Hannah," Amy's voice called. "Will you come in? You'll catch your death out there."

"I need a moment longer," Hannah replied.

The light taps of footsteps approached. "I figured you might say that."

Hannah turned to her friend and found Amy in a heavy wrap with Hannah's fur-trimmed blue cloak in her arms. Amy gave her a tender smile and lifted the garment in offering. Even as she did so, a chill rippled up Hannah's arms.

Admittedly, she *was* rather cold.

"Thank you." She took the cloak and settled it over her shoulders. It was heavy against her back, but the frigid touch of the fabric to her skin quickly warmed and blocked the worst of the wind.

Amy remained at her side for a long moment, both quiet as they gazed out at the garden where small lanterns were set up in the darkness to look like fairy lights.

"If I may…" Amy said gently.

Hannah glanced at her friend.

"What is your connection to Lord Brightstone?" A puff of frozen air fogged around Amy's heart-shaped mouth as she spoke. "You know I'll keep your secrets. But something is amiss, and I'd like to know what it is."

"I may have allowed myself to become invested in Lord Brightstone," Hannah said with a sigh.

"And why does that have you so upset?" Amy asked.

"I know my failures perfectly well." Hannah smiled weakly. "And anyway, I have no intention of marrying."

"You have no failures that I'm aware of." Amy put an arm around Hannah in a light embrace. "This isn't about our pact, is it?"

"Pact?" Hannah asked innocently, even as her heart thudded a little harder.

Amy waved her hand dismissively. "That silly pact we

made when we were at Lady Finch's. It doesn't mean none of us can ever really marry. We were practically children when we signed it."

A hard lump formed in Hannah's tumultuous stomach. She loved that pact, relished it, dreamed of the day they would finally fulfil those vows and live together in a house in the country with the freedom to do whatever they wanted. Without the judgment of the ton or the "ownership" a husband lorded over them.

Hannah's friends had never judged her. Yet even with Amy, the sweetest and best of the five of them, Hannah could not confess the true reason why she had signed the vow so long ago. The concern that she would never be wanted by a man, or be good enough to be someone's wife, had not been unfounded. Her coming out had not changed her fears but confirmed them.

To admit as much out loud, however, was far too pathetic.

Hannah gave a half-hearted laugh. "I almost forgot about the pact."

Amy smiled, visibly relieved. "I'm glad to hear it. I can't imagine that all of us wish never to wed."

Hannah hoped her smile in return appeared at least a little authentic. Was Amy the only one who felt that way about the pact? Had all the years of fantasizing about a summer cottage with her friends—free from the sting of rejection—been nothing more than a petty wish? One that would never come to be?

Suddenly, Hannah's future was as bleak as her dance prospects for the evening.

Tears pricked her eyes, and she turned from her friend, lest Amy saw the depths of her unhappiness. While Amy's gentle compassion was usually welcome, she never saw a hurt she didn't attempt to fix, and Hannah couldn't stand the possibility of having to explain why she was crying. Especially when it would only serve to make the tears fall faster.

"Would you like to return to the ball now?" Amy asked softly.

"In a moment." Hannah stared out at the cold garden, still oppressively dark despite the fairy lights. "You go ahead. I'll join you anon."

Amy squeezed her in a quick hug once more. "You know I'll come looking for you if you don't return inside soon."

Hannah nodded. She did know.

Then Amy was gone, and the silence of the night swallowed Hannah in its embrace.

The door opened again several minutes later, assaulting the quiet with the grating mix of laughter and revelry.

"You really don't have to stay out with me when it's this cold," she said without turning.

"I don't mind." The voice was familiar, but not Amy's.

Lord Brightstone.

Hannah turned around as he strode toward her with something bundled in his arms.

"What are you doing out here?" she asked.

"I saw you go outside without your cloak," he replied. "I wanted to bring it to you. And ensure there was nothing wrong."

There was something wrong. Horribly wrong.

But she could never admit as much when it had everything to do with him.

～

"I'm glad you obtained your cloak, Miss Bexley," Lucien said, genuinely relieved. He had tried to retrieve it for her when he'd seen her go out into the freezing night air with only her ballgown to protect her from the elements. However, the servants had been unable to locate her outerwear.

Instead, he had collected his own and ventured onto the terrace to bring it to her.

His presence there was more than keeping her from catching a chill. It was also an excuse to talk to her, to see *why* she had gone outside in the middle of winter.

"Amy brought me my cloak," Miss Bexley replied. "Uh, rather, Miss Honeyfield. I appear to have a good many people in my life, ensuring I don't freeze to death." She inclined her head with gratitude. "Thank you."

Lucien slid into his coat. "You seemed quiet at supper," he said, not leaving.

"Lord Ecklesby isn't especially a conversationalist with whom I prefer to engage with if I'm being honest," she replied. "We are often dining companions. I think people assume he will keep me from talking."

Lucien knew the older earl to be extraordinarily intelligent but was uncertain about his engagements with those around him. "Are they correct?"

She gave a mirthless chuckle. "Yes. I suppose it's a good strategy."

"Is that what is amiss with you?" Lucien asked, finally broaching the topic.

The golden lights behind her highlighted her cheekbones and slender, arched brows with elegant shadows as she stared at him. "I beg your pardon?"

"I believe something has upset you," he admitted. "I wanted

to see what it was. And if I could offer my assistance." All at once, he felt it might have been improper to come outside with her and that his presence was unwanted. "Is something troubling you?"

She shook her head.

He frowned, confident that was not the truth but not inclined to call her a liar to obtain it. "I'm here if you ever do wish to talk."

She nodded silently, confirming his suspicions.

"I meant to tell you earlier that I truly appreciated the book." He stepped closer, longing to have a real conversation once more this evening. Only now he knew she was the only one with whom he enjoyed conversations.

Whatever hope he'd harbored of engaging with other ladies sank lower and lower with each dance. He'd tried his hand at the weather and fashion and endured their gossip. He'd asked after the ladies often. Hannah had been correct that ladies preferred to speak at length on their opinions. While there were no uncomfortable lulls in the discussions while dancing, they were all painfully boring.

On several occasions, he had even attempted to discuss his interest in astronomy, but the response he received was feigned with pasted smiles. Then Lady Alison had insisted on a second dance, which no doubt set the gossips into a tizzy.

"I'm glad you liked your gift." The tension eased somewhat from her face as the topic moved away from her troubles. "Did you read the first volume yet?"

"I confess, I'm in the middle of another book now but intend to delve into *Pride and Prejudice* once I finish."

"What book are you reading?" she asked. Her full focus on

him suggested her query wasn't merely for the sake of filling conversation but out of sincere curiosity.

Except if he confessed the subject matter to her, she would think him stodgy. Hell, he was stodgy—he knew that. And he'd never once cared. At least until now. "Most would consider it a stuffy book," he hedged.

She laughed, appearing more like herself. "What is it about?"

He shrugged, suddenly feeling somewhat self-conscious. His interaction with Miss Bexley had been so smooth and easy since that day at the broken fence, and he hoped not to be disappointed with her displeasure at his interests now. "The stars."

Her head fell back as she gazed up at the sky. "What about them?"

"Do you see the brightest star up there?"

"That one?" She pointed to the wrong flickering glow in the distance.

"No, this one." He stepped forward, so their shoulders were next to one another. As he indicated the glowing white star, he caught her tantalizing fragrance and discreetly breathed her in, savoring her perfume and the warm nearness of her at his side.

"I see it," she said eagerly.

"Do you know what it's called?"

She looked up at him, her face only inches from his. Her mouth was so damn close to his that he had to force his eyes from that full bottom lip and how very much he should like to run his tongue along it as he kissed her.

"No, I don't know what the star is called." Her soft voice broke the spell. "Do you?"

He cleared his throat and looked up once more. "Sirius. You can tell which one it is because Orion's Belt seems to point to it."

"Sirius." She tilted her head to study the sky once more and her curled hair brushed against his shoulder. "What a curious name."

It was all he could do to keep from reaching out and letting his fingers stroke the coppery coils of her hair. "It's Greek for scorching since it glows so fervently in the night sky."

"Fascinating," she breathed. "And what is O'Bryan's Belt?"

"Orion," he gently corrected. "Do you see those three stars there, just above and to the right of Sirius, that appear to be stacked in a neat row with one another?"

She exhaled with a laugh of excitement. "I see it. Is Orion Greek as well?"

"He is," Lucien replied.

Hannah glanced up at him, her gaze somewhat coquettish. "But why his belt?"

"He was a hunter, one immortalized by the Gods to hold a place in the night sky."

"Why?" Hannah asked as she regarded the night sky, thoroughly fascinated in a way that delighted Lucien.

His fears of boring her had been groundless.

"Orion was son to a king's daughter and the sea god, Poseidon," Lucien continued. "Orion was purported to be immensely handsome and a great hunter, but he made the mistake of claiming he would kill all the animals on earth, and so Gaia, the mother of earth, created a scorpion, which stung him and killed him."

Hannah gasped. "That's terrible."

"Then you may not like the ending of the story."

She turned her wide blue eyes from the stars and toward him once more. "Do tell."

"There is another constellation you cannot see when Orion's Belt is visible, and that is Scorpius."

"The scorpion," she guessed.

Lucien nodded, unable to pull his gaze from the way the light caressed her smooth skin. "For all eternity, Orion will stalk the scorpion in the winter and run away in fear in the summer. It is said Zeus elevated them into the sky to remind mortals not to be too proud."

Her lashes cast in long shadows over her cheeks, her lips gently parted. "That's awful," she whispered.

But neither of them were looking at the stars anymore. They were both fixed on one another as if there were no sky overhead or ground at their feet. As if the ball behind them did not exist, and neither did any excuse not to touch her. Kiss her. His heart thundered like a drum against his ribs.

"Terrible," he agreed in a low murmur.

Her chin notched slightly higher as she closed her eyes. He reached for her, touching her cheek with his hands, loathing the gloves he wore.

But it was not merely his touch on her bare skin that he wanted. He lowered his head to hers and let their lips touch. Though her chin was as cold as the surrounding air, her mouth was hot and plush, the whisper of lemonade on her lips and something else...

Brandy?

He swept the tip of his tongue over the fullness of her bottom lip, and her mouth opened, yielding to him. A rush of heat suffused his body, and a sudden urgency claimed him, desperate to grab her to him, to crush her sweet curves against the hardness swelling at his loins.

While he managed to quell such temptation, he couldn't stop himself from brushing his tongue against hers. She gasped softly, and he knew he had gone too far. He immediately drew away, stepping back and putting a fair amount of distance between them even as he glanced to the doors to ensure no one had seen them.

"Forgive me, Miss Bexley. I shouldn't have taken advantage of you in such a manner." His apology came out at the same time she said, "I shouldn't have...I'm so..."

They laughed, and she ducked her head down with a sudden shyness that left him wanting to pull her to him again.

"Please, call me Hannah," she said. "But I ought to return inside. Before I'm missed. My mother..." She rolled her eyes, letting the gesture speak for her.

"If you'll call me Lucien." He came forward. "Shall I escort you inside?"

She stopped him with the shake of her head. "It might be best to go in alone, given how long we've been out here." She pressed her lips together as though savoring the reminder of their kiss.

Or perhaps he was hoping she was, the same as him.

He nodded. "Yes, of course. Good evening, Hannah."

"Good evening...Lucien." With that, she departed the terrace, her slippers silent on the cold stone as she left him alone beneath a canopy of stars. He hesitated there a moment, unable to stifle his lack of enthusiasm to return indoors where ladies would crowd him in the hopes of a dance.

Already he was tired of it all: the attention, the dancing and the dull conversations. He wanted to spend the rest of his evening with Hannah if he could free himself for a moment to do so.

In the end, it was the hope of seeing her that lured him back into the ballroom with its gilded candlelight and far too many single women. But it was to his great disappointment that he realized that Hannah was nowhere to be found.

She had left the ball.

8

A blank sheet of paper sat before Hannah, her quill at the ready in an inkwell her father had given her on her twentieth birthday.

The dinner party at her house would be that evening with Lord and Lady Whimbly, Lord and Lady Hasselton, and, of course, Lord Brightstone.

Lucien.

He had not responded to the invite until two days' ago, citing the envelope had been misplaced. Hannah did not have to guess who the cause of the lost post might be.

She could far too easily recall the look on his mother's face that night of the ball at Elizabeth's home, as surely as she could remember the kiss she'd shared with Lucien.

A shuddered exhale escaped her lips and made the paper flutter lightly on the table's polished surface.

All at once, she was drawn back on the terrace beneath a starlit sky with Lord Brightstone standing close to her, the rumble of his voice in his chest seeming to vibrate against the back of her arm. His voice was a rich timbre in her ear as he regaled her with the stories of the constellations and pointed out their locations.

It had all been fascinating and somehow strangely intimate.

And exceedingly romantic.

Heavens, now she sounded like her mother. But truly, it had been.

She loved that he knew the names of the stars and the stories behind them. Whatever he had assumed to be stodgy, she had discovered to be incredibly interesting.

Like him.

His recurrent protests of not getting on well with the opposite sex were unsupported. Every interaction they'd shared had been enjoyable and entertaining. Certainly, he had not lacked female companionship at the Langford ball. Most likely, he'd continued to be popular, though she had managed to excuse herself from the last three social events.

Citing a terrible headache, she'd been allowed to retire to bed early each night rather than attend the balls she could not summon the spirit to attend. Only it wasn't her head that ached. No, the true source was slightly lower—in her chest.

Lying in bed with the lights snuffed out was where she fully allowed herself to live in the moment of that kiss with the heat of Lucien's mouth on hers, the tease of his tongue surprising and thrilling against her lips.

She shouldn't have liked it so much, and yet how could she not?

It wasn't her first kiss. There had been one other, not long after she'd come out, a man who apparently sampled but never settled. She was fortunate to have only lost a kiss.

Rumor had it, another debutante that year had lost her reputation.

Lucien's kiss had been far more decadent than Lord Soothton's. But she still recalled how the simple kiss with Soothton had settled in her heart and blossomed into a powerful infatuation for the man. She also recollected how painful that fledgling bloom was to uproot when he ceased being interested the following day.

Every man she had ever thought to consider for a husband had hurt her, using her for one reason or another. At least Lucien was honest in what he wanted from her. Advice and direction in obtaining a wife.

That was exactly what she had agreed to give him, and she would. Which was why she was compiling this list, empty though it might be at present. But she intended to fill it with eligible young ladies who would be ideal for Lucien to marry.

Once he was bundled off to another woman, she could liberate her heart of this strange heaviness and move on with her life. She only hoped not everyone felt the way Amy did about the vow they had made at Lady Finch's and that Hannah could at least still anticipate a future in the country with some of her closest friends.

Hannah hissed an aggravated sigh and took up her quill. Lady Alison had appeared interested in him. Too much so, considering how much she fluttered her lashes at him—one would think there was a bit of lint perpetually in her eye.

She was such a wretched woman, though. To subject Lucien to her seemed unfair. But then, she *was* well off and from a good family.

A drop of ink dripped from the quill and landed in a black splatter on the page.

Heavens, but this was harder than writing the letter to him when she'd gifted him the first volume of *Pride and Prejudice*. She set the quill in the inkwell with a plink.

And to even think about him kissing Lady Alison—his warm lips on hers, soft and gentle—was enough to make Hannah want to fling the inkwell across the room. The clean scent of his shaving soap that would embrace her as it had Hannah that night under the stars.

Hannah crumpled the note, tossed it forcefully into the small bin by her desk and then took out a fresh page. This time, she wrote Lady Alison's name at the top, followed by Miss Closewell and several others. Each name Hannah wrote swiftly and without thought, before she allowed herself to acknowledge the myriad reasons to strike them off.

And there were a great many.

Lucien would doubtless be happy with any of these women, and *she* would be free once more to focus on her future as a spinster.

The door to her room opened, and Mary stepped in. "Miss Bexley, are you ready to dress for the dinner party?"

Hannah blew on the page to dry the ink and folded it in half before nodding to her maid. "Yes, I am as ready as I ever will be."

"We must have you looking your very best. Mary rushed about the room, plucking through ribbons and jewelry as she muttered to herself, her cheeks flushed.

"I think you are far too eager for Lord Brightstone's arrival," Hannah told the other woman.

Mary paused, quirked an eyebrow and straightened. "Are you not excited? Have I misread your interest in Lord Brightstone?"

"I am merely helping him if you recall." Hannah put her back to her maid so she could begin to style Hannah's thick red hair.

Mary ran the brush through the long tresses with her usual care. "Your mother thinks there may be more there between you two," she said diplomatically.

Hannah didn't answer.

"There *could* be more there," Mary added as she thrust a pin into Hannah's hair to secure it.

No matter how light one's touch was, pins always managed to stab and jab the scalp and it was miserably uncomfortable.

"I think I've been disappointed enough over the years," Hannah said with finality.

A pin fell from Mary's mouth and fell with a plop on the lush carpet. "You're not giving up, are you, dearest Hannah?"

Dearest Hannah. It was the endearing term Mary had used when Hannah was a girl and one that she still used on occasion when there was a point to make.

Hannah dropped her gaze to avoid Mary's heartbroken stare in the mirror. "I think you're becoming as dramatic as my mother."

"Maybe I want to see you happy," Mary retorted, adding another wretched pin.

"I will be." Hannah's attention slid toward the letter. "Soon."

But even as her gaze lingered on the list of names, her thoughts drifted toward Lord Brightstone. *Lucien.*

That kiss.

She need only get through this one night, present him with

a selection of potential brides all ripe for a successful match, and she could escape his allure.

Or so she thought until she saw him downstairs that evening when he arrived for dinner in a well-tailored suit of midnight blue that made her wish to stare up at the sky with him and kiss until the stars danced around them.

But no matter how much she longed to relive that night once more, in her heart, she knew it would be best to see him off and be done with it.

To finally be free of the Earl of Brightstone.

LUCIEN HAD EAGERLY ANTICIPATED the dinner party at Westwich House since he discovered the invitation lying on the floor behind the hutch in the morning room three days prior. The mistake was one he knew his butler had not made. The old man was far too careful in his years of service to the Lambert family.

The tucked-away envelope was the work of Lady Brightstone, whose sharp, disapproving gaze followed Lucien out the door that evening. It was a stare he pointedly ignored.

Now, he strode into the pale blue drawing room of Hannah's home, where candles lit against polished sconces filled the room with a golden glow. Nervous energy consumed him, making his palms overly warm in his gloves and restlessness burning in his muscles.

How many times had he thought of this exact moment in the last few days? Whatever the large number was, it was surpassed by how often he recalled that most wondrous kiss beneath the sky's brightest star. He had hoped to see Hannah again at the next ball, but when she hadn't shown, he'd assumed her absence would be for only one night.

Yet, no matter which ball or soiree or dinner party he'd attended, she was not there. He'd even chanced approaching Miss Honeyfield once, who confirmed Hannah had been unwell.

The door opened to the drawing room, and the family entered. Lord and Lady Westwich in fine dining attire and Miss Bexley—*Hannah*—in a lovely white gown accented with gold thread and beads. Her hair was carefully pinned up, revealing her slim, elegant neck that he suddenly wondered after its texture, how warm and smooth such sensitive skin might be against the whisper of his lips.

Lucien approached his hosts and bowed in greeting before taking Hannah's hand and bestowing a chaste kiss on the back of her glove.

"Lord Brightstone, it's so good of you to join us," Lady Westwich said congenially.

Lord Westwich opened his mouth to say something, but his wife nudged him along with a wide smile tossed in Lucien's direction as they left him alone with Hannah.

"I heard you were unwell." He searched her face for evidence of having been ill, but her complexion was as rosy as always. "Are you fully recovered?"

"I am, thank you." She stared at him for a long moment, and a silence that he didn't mind at all fell between them.

It was the kind of quiet one reveled in, which did not occupy one's attention to compose words but left the mind free to explore exactly what stood in front of them. That shared experience allowed him to appreciate her beauty in all its glory. The way her red curls were softer in this intimate setting, more natural, how the beads of her gown reflected the light with every subtle inhale until he could practically feel her breathing by the ripple of glittering beads. How he could still taste lemonade and brandy when his gaze found her lips.

She swallowed, and a flick of her eyes to the floor suggested her nerves were getting the better of her. "I have—"

"I've missed your company," he said earnestly at the same time she began to speak.

They laughed together, shy and nervous at once in a titillating rush of excitement. "Please, do go ahead," he said.

Whatever warm emotion was in her gaze shifted, then hardened somewhat as she reached for the reticule at her side. "I have something for you."

"Is it the second volume of *Pride and Prejudice*?"

A smile flashed uneasily on her lovely mouth. "No, I wager it will be some time before you ever read the first."

Before he could protest that he had indeed already read it and purchased the second volume, Hannah rushed on. "It is a list of eligible ladies with whom I believe you could make a suitable match."

He stilled at her words as she pulled her small, beaded purse from her wrist, the gold flecks winking in the light.

The kiss had changed nothing.

What he had been so profoundly impacted by, what they had shared that night, had changed nothing.

Of course, it had not. What an imbecile he'd been to assume it might have. They carried on so well with one another. Their banter was so smooth and effortless, their attraction so undeniable with the spark of that kiss.

Or perhaps it had been one-sided, the same as his affection. Unrequited.

He had never fancied he might be such a romantic fool, but it appeared he was indeed just that type of fool when it came to Hannah.

She fumbled with her reticule a moment, the delicate clasp slipping against her gloves before she snapped it open and handed him a folded paper.

He hesitated to accept it, and the parchment shivered between the pinch of her fingers. Was she as loath to present it to him as he was to receive it, or was he simply injecting emotion where there was none on her part?

Perhaps the kiss had been the same way. Perhaps she had not wanted it but did not wish to be rude when he'd leaned over her. A sinking feeling rolled in his stomach. "I should apologize—"

"Here." She pushed the list into his hand.

Wordlessly, he accepted the paper from her and unfolded it.

Lady Alison headed the list, the vapid young woman who feigned her laughter with delicate titter that grated at his nerves and fluttered her lashes like a doe in a blizzard. The gossip wrought by the second dance she had insisted on still haunted him. He immediately tossed aside the idea of even fathoming a future with so detestable a woman.

Next came Miss Closewell, a name that sounded familiar but one he could not place. On and on, the list went until fifteen young women from esteemed families were noted. And not one of them was Miss Hannah Bexley.

The butler entered the room at that exact moment, saving Lucien from having to compose a response. Instead, he refolded the note and thrust it into his jacket pocket, where it rested like a boulder against his heart.

"We'll be sitting beside one another, of course," Hannah said. "To ensure I can give you proper guidance on polite dinner conversation."

The sinking sensation in his stomach crashed down to his toes. This was why he had been invited to a dinner party at Westwich Place. Not to be part of an intimate family gathering where he and Hannah might speak to one another in a more private setting, but so that she could further instruct him.

At least his mother would be happy.

They made their way to the dining room, where the table had been set with polished silver and an array of hothouse flowers. His seat was by Hannah's, naturally, framed by the rest of the attendees. There would be no opportunity to speak alone. Yet the press of his inexcusable kiss was almost suffocating him.

"If I caused you offense on our last meeting, I truly do apologize," he said in a low voice that others would not be likely to hear.

"There was no offense taken," Hannah replied quietly.

He tried to read her expression, which was curiously blank despite her reddening cheeks. "This list…"

"It's what I'm here for." She smiled brightly at him. Perhaps too brightly. "To help you in your marital pursuits."

He frowned. "What happened that night—"

"Can't happen again," she said quickly.

The swiftness of her reply confirmed his suspicions that his advances had been entirely unwelcome, and he had egregiously misread what lay between them.

"Forgive me my misstep." He met her gaze, earnest to his soul. "I can assure you that it will not."

Hannah gave a prim nod as the first course was served, a delicate white soup favored at most dinner parties but not much to his liking. Lifting her spoon, she said, "Discussing what you are eating is always a good topic of conversation."

Lucien nodded and prepared himself for a night of careful instruction, though he suddenly found his role in the game tiresome. Through his lessons to become desirable among the ton, he realized it was not the material that enticed him but the tutor.

If nothing else, he would at least be equipped with the tools necessary to find a wife as the lady whose company he had come to enjoy continued to remain out of reach.

9

$\mathcal{A}$s the dinner party pressed on, Lucien was exceedingly aware that, despite Hannah's protests he had not caused offense, he most assuredly had. Or at least, it was the only explanation he could summon for her incredibly cordial manner.

But it did not make him wish to escape her company. Rather, he wished they might be alone for him to apologize properly. A chance he was well aware would not be possible. The most he could hope for would be a private card game between them sometime later when they reconvened in the drawing room.

As their plates of marzipan cakes and sliced oranges were cleared away, Lord Westwich addressed them all. "At this time, I would invite the gentlemen to join me for port as the ladies retire to the drawing room."

Hannah rose with the other ladies and departed, but not before casting one last, lingering look in his direction. It was the prolonged gaze that most confused him, for it was one of yearning and heartbreak. Granted, he was no expert on women, or he would never have needed her instruction in the first place. But recently, he had become exceedingly aware of the emotion and how it might affect someone viscerally.

Namely him.

And, as he'd once hoped, her as well.

"Lord Brightstone." Lord Westwich settled at the open seat beside Lucien and waved a servant over with the port decanter. Lord Hasselton and Lord Whimbly were already discussing Napoleon's recent imprisonment on Saint Helena, where the landscape was said to be less than hospitable.

"Tell me, what do you make of this Elgin Marble business?" Westwich said as the servant carefully poured a measure of rich red wine into first Lucien's empty glass, then that of Lord Westwich.

The marble statues the baron referred to had been on the tongue of every member of Parliament since the season began. The marbles had been excavated from the Parthenon in Greece by the Earl of Elgin by somewhat questionable means.

"I believe we ought to await the evidence to ensure the items were procured honorably," Lucien answered with his usual diplomatic decorum.

Westwich chuckled. "I believe you have stronger feelings than that. My daughter told me of your love for history."

Lucien masked his surprise at this, but only just. He hadn't expected Hannah to speak of him to her parents, let alone in praise.

"It's true." He set aside civility with his host for a more candid response. "If the marbles were obtained under false pretenses, it would be a travesty to Greek culture and a mark against England to have allowed such an atrocity to befall so sacred a place."

Westwich nodded. "From what I understand, they have not been well cared for in the time they've been in Elgin's ownership, moldering away in ill-kept storage."

"Better to have left them where they belonged than subject them to such treatment." Lucien sipped his port to keep from becoming too passionate on a topic he vehemently felt for. There was a certain *laissez-faire* attitude toward the history of other countries that crossed into pillaging, and he did not condone it in the least.

"Speaking of precious treasures…" Lord Westwich lifted a brow. "What are your intentions toward my daughter?"

The port slipped down Lucien's throat wrong, caught with a startled inhale. He coughed, sputtering more than he would have liked when faced with such a question.

Westwich clapped him on the back with a laugh. "Come now, my boy, I want you to be honest with me. Lady Westwich and I cannot help but notice how much time the two of you have spent together. Yet you have not once sought me out to ask my permission to court her. I know you can be somewhat…odd." He held up his hands. "Respectfully."

Lucien was not at all offended, not after the years of rumors he'd heard about himself.

"While this is, admittedly, somewhat unconventional," Lord Westwich continued, "I wished to approach you on the matter in case you did not feel comfortable coming to me."

Lucien took another sip of wine, this one somewhat larger. At least the gulp went down smoother than the last.

"Well?" Lord Westwich gave a good-natured smile, his easy

spirit reminiscent of Hannah's. "What have you to say, my lord?"

"I…" Lucien stammered. "That is to say…that I…"

Westwich chortled and patted Lucien on the shoulder. "Out with it. Surely, it cannot be so difficult to say what is going on between the two of you."

"You have an extraordinarily kind daughter," Lucien spoke slowly as his mind raced to piece together carefully a proper explanation.

Westwich grinned and nodded.

"She has a sharp wit and is exceptionally fashionable," Lucien continued.

A twinkle touched Westwich's deep blue eyes. "Indeed, she does."

In that moment, Lucien wished he had asked for the earl's permission to court Hannah. Not only to appeal to the man's obvious pride, but also for Lucien's own desires. He wanted Hannah above all other women in England. Certainly, more than any of those ladies on that damnable list.

That look of longing she'd cast him as she left billowed forefront in Lucien's thoughts again. But he could no sooner put her in such a position as to be forced to be courted by him than he could steal another unwanted kiss from her.

"She has been assisting me this season," Lucien finally confessed.

"Assisting?" The smile remained on Westwich's face, though his brows furrowed in slight confusion. "Is that a strange turn of phrase? You youth are so creative with your own vernacular these days."

"It is assisting in the sense with which you are familiar." Lucien cleared his throat, mortified to admit the truth aloud to another person, most especially Hannah's father. "You see, Miss Bexley has been assisting me on my wardrobe purchases and offering guidance on what to say while dancing and at dinner parties. Such as the fine one you hosted this evening."

The confusion on Lord Westwich's face fully replaced any affability in his expression now. "I don't understand."

"She has been helping me become more appealing to others." Lucien sipped his wine again. "To women."

The older earl shook his head. "Why would she do this?"

Lucien sighed. "So that I might attract a wife."

Lord Westwich's face darkened to a strange shade of russet. "She is helping you be more fashionable so that you might court and wed someone else," he said in summary. "But not my daughter."

There was a glint in his eye, but it was not jovial as before. It was somewhat murderous.

Lucien nodded slowly.

"You have been occupying her at every social event thus far this season." Westwich's nostrils flared. "So that you could find someone else to marry. And what of my daughter and her prospects?"

It was not Lucien's place to tell Westwich of Hannah's decision not to wed. Lucien clenched his back teeth, knowing exactly how much of a cad this entire scenario made him seem.

"And what of my Hannah?" Westwich declared. "Is she not good enough for you?"

"She is uninterested." At least in this, Lucien could be honest.

"I've seen you at the soirees and balls this week." West-wich's jaw tightened. "In your fashionably cut jackets, amid a crowd of swooning ladies. It appears my daughter's efforts were successful. Which means you may now leave her be to the suitors she deserves rather than spending any more time with your wasted companionship."

Lucien wanted to protest, to resolve a way to remain in Hannah's presence. But no matter her future intentions, her father was right. It was unfair for Lucien to continue to occupy her company when there was no opportunity for a marital agreement between them.

While she did not desire to be a wife, she could well meet someone at a ball who would unexpectedly sweep her off her feet, much in the way Darcy seemed to have done with Elizabeth Bennett.

The very idea of it squeezed at a tender place in Lucien's chest. But he would not begrudge her an opportunity for a happy life in love, nor would he prevent her from it.

"I will not trouble Miss Bexley any further," Lucien said.

Lord Westwich narrowed his eyes. "I have your word as a gentleman?"

Lucien nodded. "You do."

And from that moment on, he vowed to himself to never even think of venturing beyond the civil edicts of society with Miss Bexley again. Not after having caused so much discontent.

DINNER HAD BEEN utter torture for Hannah. Lucien appeared vexed by the list of potential brides, but was that not why he'd sought her out initially?

She took a sip of tea, barely listening to her mother's

discussion with Lady Whimbly and Lady Hasselton on which silk thread was best to use for embroidery. This was interspersed with a bit of gossip about a new debutante who placed herself in a rather precarious situation with Lady Arksford's grandson.

So much for propriety.

Time with Lucien was something Hannah had always anticipated with relish. But tonight, their interaction had been limited to the edification of polite dinner conversation. She instructed, and he listened.

The façade had been taxing to maintain, but she had not been able to stop herself from looking back as she left, to gaze at what a handsome figure he cut one last time. What would it be like to be a normal courting couple with Lucien? One where he was genuinely interested in her for who she actually was and not what she could do for him.

An ache clenched in her heart.

The doors to the drawing room opened, and the men entered. Lucien was beside her father, his strong jaw set as his cerulean eyes met hers. A jolt of energy shot through her, making her pulse jump.

"Forgive me, but I must take my leave," he announced to Hannah's mother.

The cards tumbled from Lady Westwich's hands. "Oh, I'm so terribly sorry to hear it." She swept to her feet, heedlessly scattering the dropped cards as she approached him. "We do hope to have you come again sometime soon."

Lucien bowed to her and turned to Hannah. His hair was slightly overgrown, in need of a trim. It reminded her of when she'd first met him, with his shaggy hair and the comfortable, loose garb of a tutor rather than an earl. She missed that shy scholar who had first approached her to help him become more desirable.

"I hope you are not unwell," Hannah said politely.

He shook his head. "I apologize for my abrupt departure."

No further explanation was offered, and in such a formal setting, it would be impolite to push him for more information. She had led him to assume his kiss had offended her. And while it had been painful and unkind for her to do so, the falsehood had been necessary for her own sanity.

If he kissed her again, she did not know that she could guard her heart against his charms any longer. Allowing herself to love him as she'd once thought to love others would be too hard to overcome when he rejected her.

And he would.

They all did.

Especially when he had so many attractive, sought-after women vying for his attention.

She nodded. "Thank you for joining us."

He bowed. "I appreciate the invite and the instruction." His mouth flattened into a hard line. "And the list."

That blasted list. The mere mention of it set her teeth on edge. "It was my pleasure," she said, practically choking on the words. For it had not been a pleasure—the arduous task had been miserable as she imagined him with each of those women.

"I bid you a good evening, Miss Bexley," he said with a formality they'd never shared. "And farewell."

The way he met her eyes as he spoke and the sincerity with which the statement was delivered somehow felt as though he was not simply bidding her farewell that evening but forever.

A knot stuck fast in her throat, and she excused herself not long afterward, unable to concentrate on the cards in her hand. How could she when instead she continued to think upon the list and how he might win over any one of those ladies?

The following day, she expected some kind of letter from Lucien, some way to explain his abrupt departure. None came.

While the night before, she'd sought this solitude as a break from him, a chance to recover her wits, it now fell over her like a weight. His coldness made her desperate to revisit his warmth, and the distance had her craving his closeness.

Jillian's father was to host a ball in a week, one of the grandest of the season, or so it was rumored. For her part, Jillian did not care, as it was to be an announcement of her betrothal to the Duke of Dudley. Or, as she called it, the death knell.

Everyone who was anyone in London society would be there, meaning Lucien would also be in attendance.

Except that the ball was another week away. Hannah flopped dramatically on her bed. How could she possibly wait an entire week to see him again?

Of course, there was still another volume of *Pride and Prej-udice* to send him, which would require a note. It was the perfect opportunity for a reason to write him and—better still —one for him to respond.

Even as she knew she should not, that she ought to embrace his chilly silence, she sent a servant to obtain a copy of the second volume while she set to work writing a missive.

If there had been a pile of wadded paper before, the heap

was a veritable tower now. At last, she had the perfect thing to say. Or so she hoped.

Lucien,

I trust this gift finds you much recovered from whatever ailed you at our dinner party. It was good of you to attend, and our conversation was enjoyable as always. I anticipate seeing you at Lady Jillian's ball next week, but in the meantime, I thought you might enjoy the next volume in Pride and Prejudice. *I look forward to hearing your thoughts on the story.*

With sincerity,

Hannah

Perhaps it had been bold to use their Christian names, but it felt right to do so. That and she wanted to heighten the intimacy with the familiar names even as she was aware, deep down, she should refrain.

She held onto the book and the note for an entire day before finally giving them to Mary and hastening her maid from the room to deliver them before she changed her mind. An act she immediately regretted once she knew they were likely in his hands.

The knowledge was bittersweet. She had done it, nudging the exchange between them into motion once more. And yet, she was plagued by fear every moment thereafter.

The wait for a reply from Lucien was interminable. It did not arrive that afternoon, but the following morning after breakfast, Mary entered the room with something tucked behind her back.

Hannah's heart missed a beat as she bolted upright, the book she'd been reading flung aside in her haste without an opportunity to note the page number. "Have I received a response from Lord Brightstone? Why did Jones not deliver it at breakfast this morning with the rest of my father's correspondence?"

Mary's face fell. "You will not like what I've brought you."

Hannah shook her head, not understanding. At least, not until Mary approached the bed and withdrew what she had been holding behind her back. It was the second volume of *Pride and Prejudice* and Hannah's note to Lucien.

She took both with trembling hands and turned the envelope, revealing the seal was still intact. He hadn't been bothered to break the thick layer of wax. The letter she had painstakingly worded had not even been read.

The rejection of her gift stung as viscerally as she'd expected it would. This was why the letter never ought to have been sent in the first place. And why she should never have placed herself in such a place of vulnerability.

The pain was deep and unforgiving, where it lodged in her chest like fire.

It was not simply the sorrow of imagining never again being kissed by him or experiencing his strong embrace as they danced. The loss was truly for the man himself. For his sweet, shy, awkward nature, for the knowledge he possessed, and the way conversation flowed so readily between them.

At that moment, she realized that she would rather have Lucien as a friend than not have him in her life at all.

10

Hannah took more care than usual when preparing to attend Jillian's ball the following week. She wore a new ice-blue silk gown with a bodice and hem that glinted with small crystals and flowers embroidered with silver thread. Her hair was twisted, pinned and curled with a hot tong until she was the very picture of top fashion.

Her efforts were acknowledged in the squealing compliments from her friends. However, her enjoyment of their affectionate encouragement was dampened by realizing how much they did not know about what had so recently transpired in her life.

Yes, they had teased her about the time she spent with Lucien. Yes, Lucy alluded to Hannah's hand in helping establish his new fashionable presence.

But none of them knew about the kiss, nor how desperately Hannah longed for him to be interested in her, nor even of her fears of rejection. Fears that were realized again and again each season with yet another gentleman whose interest she had placed too high a wager on.

Jillian looked radiant in a white silk gown with a sparkling silver tissue that made her catch the candlelight like a star.

Sirius.

The brightest star in the sky.

The newfound fact of the heavens dawned on Hannah before she could stop it, followed by the memory of Lucien's warm lips upon hers and how her heart had nearly pounded out of her chest.

"Lady Jillian." The Duke of Dudley appeared at her side. "I should like to dance this first set together."

Jillian turned to him with a pretty smile hovering on the corners of her lips. "Would you dance with me if I was a tree?"

He sighed, not bothering to stifle his irritation. "How could I possibly dance with you if you were a tree?"

She tilted her face as if the chandeliers overhead were sunlight. "To the sway of the wind, and the orchestra the rustling leaves and birdsong."

As if on cue, the opening notes of the first dance began to tinkle to life.

"Don't be preposterous," the duke grated out in a low hiss. "This foolishness must cease. Come, we are to open your ball with a dance." He extended his hand to her, which she slowly accepted.

She was whisked away from them before they could protest. There was something extraordinarily awful about having seen such a display. It was more than a man crushing the spirit of a woman; it was Jillian's spirit he sought to destroy. Everything colorful and beautiful and fascinatingly unique about who she was had dulled at that moment. After a lifetime of such treatment, that beautiful light that was Jillian's creative soul might eventually wink out.

Hannah and the other three women were silent as they watched Jillian gracefully take her place on the dance floor.

"I hate that there isn't more we can do to stop this," Elizabeth said softly.

"I could find a way," Lucy said with a curl of her lips.

"Don't you dare," Amy warned half-heartedly before sighing in quiet resignation. "What did you have in mind?"

But Lucy wasn't listening. She was craning her neck across the room to where a crowd of women bustled around something.

Hannah looked in the same direction. Her stomach dropped, and she realized it wasn't *something* but *someone*.

And that someone was Lucien.

A jewel-toned array of ballgowns swished and swirled as women tried to get closer to him. He bestowed smile after devastating smile to his adoring devotees.

Whatever ached in Hannah's chest before, now burned like an ember, red-hot and glowing.

"Isn't that your neighbor?" Amy asked.

"It is," Hannah replied as if she did not care. But, of course, she did. Far more than she should.

But he was not out for the first dance with any of the women as she'd suspected he would be. Instead, he was walking away from the crowd of eligible ladies.

At least now would present a chance to speak to him.

"Excuse me," Hannah mumbled and quickly swept through the crowds toward him.

As she neared Lucien, however, he shifted, moving in the opposite direction. At first, she thought this was simply a coincidence until she redirected her steps, and he once more altered his.

He was intentionally evading her.

The realization struck her like a slap.

He was fleeing from her.

Suddenly, she understood the situation for exactly what it was. He had all he needed from her. All the time they had spent together—he had gleaned the proper way to dress, the courage to lead ladies onto the dance floor and how to best converse with them. In those three small areas, he had gone from a man oft overlooked to a man most sought after. He had done so through her counsel and guidance.

And now, there was no further need of her in his life.

It was so painfully clear that the ache she felt earlier rose and lodged in her throat.

On the dance floor, the Duke of Dudley led Jillian in a stiff dance, his face as stern as his sense of humor. And all the while, poor Jillian's chin remained up and her posture proud. Her lips were moving as she spoke, and the duke's face seemed to darken. Doubtless, Jillian had not stifled "her foolishness," as the duke had called it, and the victory of her friend's defiance made Hannah proud.

If only she could be as strong as Jillian, who did not care what she said, nor to whom, Hannah would approach Lucien over the matter rather than let his rejection wither her spirit.

And what was stopping her?

Nothing.

Nothing stopped her from marching across the ballroom until Lucien had no place to go and confronting him with the truth of her anger toward him. Decision locked thoroughly in place, she set across the room like a warship locked on its target.

As she drew closer to Lucien, he skirted away. She pursued.

Finally, when they were nearing a wall, he turned to face her. "Ah, Miss Bexley, what a lovely surprise."

"My presence before you is no more of a surprise than you are a gentleman," she whispered in a low voice to keep from being overheard. It was not her intention to dishonor him but to explain how rude his actions were and that she would not tolerate his indifference.

She would never command the love and adoration that others did in life, but she at least deserved better than how she was being treated.

"You saw me heading toward you, and you attempted to run away from me." There was a wounded note in her voice she hadn't the time or energy to mask.

His shoulders sagged. "Forgive me, Miss Bexley. It isn't as it appeared."

"You mean you were not trying to escape having a conversation with me?" She frowned as she imagined how she could have been wrong when it seemed so obvious that he was avoiding her.

"No, I was." He lifted a shoulder. "Only it isn't why you think."

"I know exactly why." She crossed her arms over her chest.

"I'm so glad you understand," he replied, appearing visibly relieved.

She stepped closer, brutally aware of how many eyes would be on them if she went *too* near. "You used me. You feigned friendship to obtain the skills necessary to become popular among the ton. Now that you've achieved your goal, you have no need for me."

He gaped at her. "No, you have it all wrong."

She scoffed. "I don't think I do."

"Come outside with me a moment and allow me to explain," he replied. "I do not want to speak in here, not with such gossips in proximity."

No doubt, he didn't want people to know exactly how immoral he was in his pursuit of an elevated reputation. Suddenly, she was immensely pleased she had placed Lady Alison at the top of the list. The two so richly deserved one another.

"Please, Hannah," he said softly.

She sucked in a sharp breath and glanced around to confirm no one had witnessed him calling her by her Christian name.

"Very well," she agreed. "But only for a moment. I'll go first. You follow." Without waiting for him to respond, she turned on her heel and left him standing where she had cornered him.

Whatever he had to say ought to be entertaining if nothing else. How did he truly plan to justify his actions after he had used her through feigned friendship?

It took Lucien slightly longer than anticipated to join Hannah on the terrace. The night was as cold as the last time he had been alone at night with Hannah, and it made the memory of her so rich in his mind that he could not help but relive the moment in his imagination.

The sweet scent of her, the intoxicating taste of her lips, the desperation for so much more than a kiss, the simple intimacy. He enjoyed her company immensely and hated the week they had spent apart.

Even returning the book that she'd sent over with her card unopened had required exceptional willpower. He'd held that letter for the better part of a day, even trying to stare through the heavy cardstock to read the words inside without opening it and breaking the seal.

No matter how much he wanted to keep the gift and read the note, to do so would only encourage her friendship further. It was better to break off his acquaintanceship with her.

For her sake.

Except that the open hurt in her eyes, the way it left a slight tremor in her voice, cut him to the quick. He realized he had to be honest with her, not only about what her father had said to him but about his feelings for her.

Lucien's attempts to reach the other side of the room to the terrace doors were met with constant interruption. Half of them were women whose names graced that damned list Hannah had penned in her careful script for him. All of them were women he decidedly did *not* want.

However, the more he tried to get away, the more they seemed to chase him down, almost desperate in their need for his undivided attention. When at last he pushed onto the terrace, Hannah was standing in front of the door, her hand reaching for the latch to open it and return inside.

She backed up, slightly startled. "I didn't think you were going to come."

"Forgive me," he replied. "I was detained."

Her arms were crossed over her chest and the breath fogged from her in frozen puffs. Lucien immediately took his jacket off and placed it around her shoulders, guiding her toward a corner with a wall that would buffet the wind from them.

"Too many adoring women?" she asked through chattering teeth.

"You're freezing. We ought to return inside."

"No." She gazed up at him, her mouth hard with a stubbornness that made him want to kiss them soft again. "I want this resolved."

Lucien sighed, noting the welcome scent of her perfume on his inhale. "Have you spoken to your father?"

She frowned. "My father? What does he have to do with this?"

Unease clenched low in Lucien's belly. Lord Westwich had not divulged the details of their conversation with Hannah. However, if Lucien had to choose between Westwich and Hannah's loyalty, he would choose Hannah. Without thought, prevarication or hesitation. Always.

"My constant presence at your side is preventing suitors from pursuing you," Lucien explained.

Hannah stared at him for a long moment as his words settled over her.

"Are you serious?" she asked.

"Of course, I am."

Her gaze narrowed. "My father told you this, didn't he?"

Lucien didn't reply.

"Was this my father's doing?" Her eyes flashed with a deep anger Lucien had never seen before.

"I don't want to keep you from being approached by suitors, Hannah. I won't let you sacrifice your future for mine."

She continued to stare up at him, her expression one of bewilderment. "What suitors?"

"Precisely," he replied. "Haven't you noticed that no other men have even so much as asked you to dance in the time you've been helping me?"

"None of that matters." Her chin tilted with indignation. "I told you I have no plans to marry."

"I'm aware of this," he replied. "Though I'm not sure your father knows this, nor that he would support your decision."

"Of course, he wouldn't support it." Hannah turned away from him. Her shoulders squared with rage beneath the outline of his jacket. "He and my mother both think I deserve the sort of love they discovered with one another."

Lucien approached cautiously and set his hands on Hannah's shoulders. He wanted to grasp them and turn her back around toward him, to kiss her beneath the wide, open face of the moon until they were both breathless.

Now, he realized. He needed to tell her what she meant to him now.

"You do deserve that," Lucien said gently.

"No one believes that except my parents." She shook her head. "Least of all me."

"You might meet someone…a man who makes you come alive, who makes you feel like you are perfect exactly as you are," he said, speaking of himself and how he felt about her.

"Do you know why I want to be a spinster?"

"No, though I can't imagine a woman of your radiance ever being a spinster," he confessed. His heart pounded in anticipation for sharing with her exactly how beautiful he thought her to be. Not only her vibrance, but her wit, her appearance, her kindness and how desperately he wished she might consider being courted by him.

"My radiance," she repeated the word with unexpected cynicism. "I know my deficiencies, Lucien. I am too loud, too talkative, too much in general. I'm a hoyden."

He opened his mouth to protest, but she shook her head, stopping him. "I know what people say about me. My head is not thrust into the sand. I am the woman who is there to aid anyone requiring assistance. I'm *kind*." She threw the last word as if it was derogatory. "I'm not the woman men see and think of as a wife and a mother. I'm the woman men know will help when asked. In the years since my debut, I've been a dance partner for a man who could scarcely identify a beat for a quadrille. I've offered advice on a coming out ball for another man's sister."

Lucien recognized Lord Ranford in the small detail and recalled how the other earl had danced with Hannah before Lucien on so many nights.

"And then there's you," Hannah continued. "You asked me for my assistance in making you more fashionable. And I said yes. Because I am *kind*. Because I am the woman who says yes where I can give support. But I am never the woman who is asked to be courted."

"That isn't true." He reached for her, taking her gloved hand in his. "Allow me to court you."

She jerked her hand from his. "I beg your pardon?"

Lucien tried to reach for her again, but she stepped back from his reach. "You are so lovely and fascinating," he began, but the look of horror on her face stopped him.

"Don't," she whispered.

"Hannah, I don't want to get to know these other ladies

when I already know you so well. I can go to your father tomorrow—"

"Wouldn't that please him greatly?" she said in a harsh voice.

He gazed at her in the wash of moonlight, her skin like marble, her dress shimmering. She was stunning, a being so exquisite that she was practically otherworldly. And yet, he still preferred her in the country, with her bonnet off and her hair in a loose knot falling around her face. "Would it...please you?"

"If you asked to court me?" she asked incredulously. "No."

Her rejection was a dagger, and its pointed blade snagged a tender mark he hadn't realized was still raw in his chest. Hannah was not the first person he had asked to court. There had been Lady Cecelia Stopford, who he discovered later had been too embroiled in family affairs to spare the time to be courted.

Then there had been Lady Martha Sinclair. She had hair black as the darkest part of the night and a matching heart to pair with it. He had been young, full of foolish pursuits and lofty ideals. His interest in her had been solely for her beauty, and her cruelty had been the price extolled. When he asked if she would allow him to court her, she had laughed in his face and told him he knew little of women and would make a terrible husband.

Seeing the tears sparkle in Hannah's eyes now and how poorly he'd played his hand, he realized the truth behind those biting words. He truly did not know women. If he had, he would not have blundered things so hopelessly.

"Hannah..."

She shook her head, silencing him. "I neither want nor need your pity."

"It isn't pity."

She swept his jacket from her shoulders and thrust it toward him. "Good evening, Lord Brightstone."

And with that formal farewell, she departed the terrace, leaving him alone in the dark, desolate cold.

11

The ballroom blurred in a wash of tears as Hannah pushed back into the glowing heat inside. The pain in her chest was so great that it was difficult to breathe.

Finally, she had been asked to be courted. And it had been out of sheer pity.

Because her father had appealed to a gentleman on her behalf, claiming Lucien was drawing away her suitors. As if they would be coming in droves otherwise.

What humiliation. What misery.

She wished at that moment that she was home and could fling herself onto her bed to give in to the tears she could scarcely keep at bay. The ballroom was overly warm and made the heat in her cheeks scalding.

As if sensing a friend in need, Amy was immediately at her side. "Hannah, what is it?"

Using the last ounce of her self-control, Hannah swallowed the enormity of her hurt and faced her friend. "I have a terrible headache," she lied. "I believe it would be best if I take my leave."

Amy's kind brown gaze lingered on Hannah, skeptical. But she did not question Hannah further. Instead, she said she would notify Hannah's parents and disappeared in a swirl of russet silk. There was a cup of lemonade in her hand when she returned with Elizabeth at her side. Poor Jillian was still being occupied by the Duke of Dudley, and Lucy was on the dance floor with a devilishly handsome man none of them had seen before.

"Come, we'll take you to collect your wrap and wait for your carriage with you." Elizabeth curled an arm around Hannah in a brief embrace.

It was a small gesture of comfort that nearly collapsed Hannah's tenuous control over the tide of her emotions. She merely nodded and allowed them to guide her toward the front of the townhouse.

This was why she wanted her future to be one surrounded by the love of friends rather than that of a man. Whatever existed between her and Lord Brightstone had been exhilarating, yes, but it had also been fraught with hurt and uncertainty. And mortification.

With friends, she did not have to worry about losing herself to her emotions. She did not have to worry about rejection. And most assuredly, she did not have to worry about a proposal of courtship out of pity.

Why had her father gone to Lucien? And why had Lucien taken it upon himself to ask to court her after admitting his guilt?

It was better for her to know from the start, of course. Better than her allowing Lucien to court her, becoming further invested in his affection, then realizing later that it had all been done because he felt bad for her. Because she was so pathetic, she could not attract a husband on her own.

Fresh tears stung her eyes.

Yes, a life spent in the company of her friends would be far better than one riddled with this unending agony.

The following morning, Hannah did not feel any better. If anything, she felt far worse. A night of sobbing into her pillow left her eyes gritty and swollen, which made what she read in the scandal sheets all the more miserable.

Lucien…no, she mustn't think of him with such familiarity any longer—Lord Brightstone had officially been declared the most eligible bachelor of the season.

Lord B has been hiding in plain sight all these years and has finally allowed himself to truly be seen. The ladies are all aflutter over this blue-eyed earl whose estates include…

Hannah closed the paper and set it forcefully on the table.

"Hannah, dearest," Lady Westwich said gently. "What is the matter? First, you leave your friend's ball extremely early, your face is swollen as a modiste's pincushion, and now even the newspaper offends."

"Lord Brightstone asked me to allow him to court me last night," Hannah confessed glumly.

Her mother sat upright in her chair, her expression radiant. "Did he? But why are you…"

"He asked because Father told him to." Hannah stared at her untouched eggs rather than look at Lord Westwich.

"Henry," her mother said in a reprimanding tone. "What came over you, asking him to do such a thing?"

"I did nothing of the sort." A crinkle indicated her father had set aside his newspaper.

"He said you informed him he was chasing off my suitors."

Hannah looked up at her father, not appreciating the full depth of his betrayal until that moment.

"Well, he isn't wrong," Lady Westwich countered. "Your father said Lord Brightstone's interest in you was from a purely assistance-based need. If he is determined to wed another woman, you needn't keep him around. However, if he means to court you…"

"Because he felt sorry for me." Her voice broke.

"Come now, that isn't true," her father said gently but unconvincingly. Lord Westwich always was a horrible liar. "He genuinely likes you."

Lord Brightstone did not harbor an actual affection toward her, and her father knew it as well as she did. She wished she could say the same, that she was as indifferent to the earl as he was to her. One look at the crumpled newspaper at her side, however, made her heart squeeze so viscerally that she knew the dreaded truth.

She cared immensely for Lord Brightstone. Not the fashionable gentleman in the fitted clothing with the cropped hairstyle all the dandies sported, but the shy earl with hair long past due for a trim who cradled a frightened cat against his chest.

Yes, she was smitten yet again despite her determination to remain otherwise. What was worse, she'd created an eligible bachelor whose exploits would occupy the attention of the ton for the entirety of the season. And she would be forced to sit back and watch his success.

That afternoon, she was notified of a visitor and found Jillian downstairs waiting for her in a lovely green day dress and silk shawl.

Hannah rushed to her friend. "Jillian, I'm so sorry for

having missed so much of your ball."

"I wish I could have missed it." Jillian rolled her eyes.

"Was the duke so terrible?" Hannah poured tea carefully into both their cups and handed one to her friend, who accepted it with thanks.

Jillian stared into her teacup. "Do you ever wonder if it's possible for someone to blot out another's existence entirely?"

"Is it truly that bad?" Hannah idly stirred her tea. "Did you agree to marry him?"

"He asked. I prevaricated." Jillian shook her head. "And my father is greatly displeased. You know he is determined to see me wed. But at least it allows me a bit more time to come up with a way to get out of this mess."

Hannah nodded and didn't bother to ask how the Duke of Dudley had taken the news.

"But the dastardly duke is not why I am here." Jillian reached across the table for Hannah's hand. "I have come to visit on behalf of all of us without overwhelming you. We know you did not have a headache last night and suspect there might be more under the surface."

"Oh." Hannah busied herself selecting a tea cake she didn't have the appetite to eat.

The small confection with a red marzipan flower and delicate green leaves looked the best. Or perhaps the marigold with dots of orange framing it on the petite square?

"Does it have to do with Lord Brightstone?" Jillian asked.

Hannah grabbed the one closest to her and popped it into her mouth. "Hmm?"

Her friend gave a knowing smile. "We are all going to be in attendance at Vauxhall Gardens on Thursday and should like you to join us. We'll have use of Lord Langston's supper box, and Madame Saqui is said to be performing. I can't imagine anyone in all of London who would enjoy her tightrope performance more than you."

Hannah's disinclination to join them began to waver at the mention of the famed tightrope walker of Vauxhall Gardens. There had been much talk about the performer, but Hannah had not yet had the opportunity to see her. "You do know how to sweeten an invitation."

"I take it that's a yes." Jillian smiled and sipped her tea.

"As long as Lord Brightstone's name isn't mentioned once." Hannah leveled her gaze at her friend. "If I go, I want to remove him entirely from my thoughts and focus solely on my enjoyment with you ladies."

"Consider it done," Jillian replied with an elegant lift of her shoulder.

Hannah beamed at her friend. "In that case, an evening in Vauxhall would be delightful."

Lucien was in an uncommonly sour mood the following day after his ill-fated discussion with Hannah. Lady Martha had been correct all those years ago; he truly did not understand women.

Or at least, he'd failed to learn how to speak to them properly. In hindsight, he realized his error in confessing his feelings to her after admitting to his conversation with Lord Westwich. Now he was labeled as the season's most eligible bachelor. A title that had his mother gloating as she purposefully unearthed reasons to attend morning calls earlier that day.

The world rushed by the carriage windows as Lucien made his way to White's. At the gentleman's club, he could be ensured a reprieve from the business of matchmaking and debutantes.

His carriage drew to a stop, and he rushed out into a blustery wind that made him anticipate the strong cup of tea he intended to acquire upon entry. The massive room held the odor of stale smoke from the popular cigarillos and a lingering aroma of brandy that made him recall that kiss with Hannah.

Even here, far from his home, her memory still tugged at him with an undeniable lure. Perhaps he needed something a little stiffer than a cup of tea.

"Ah, if it isn't the season's most sought-after bachelor." The familiar voice pulled his attention to Lord Ranford, who approached with two highball glasses cupped in his large right hand, both with hearty pours of amber liquid.

"Scotch?" Ranford held one in Lucien's direction. "It doesn't seem like a day for tea."

Ah, yes. Ranford's sister had fallen in love with a man and was soon to wed. Their engagement announcement was in the same scandal sheet as the declaration of Lucien's popularity as a sought-after bachelor.

"I understand felicitations are in order." Lucien took the cut crystal glass from his friend and indicated the empty chair across from him in silent invitation.

Ranford sank into the seat with a grateful smile. "I thought she would wait several more years before finally deciding on a gentleman but am pleased she's found someone who makes her genuinely happy."

"You've always been a good brother to her." Lucien drank

his scotch and let the pleasant burn slide down into his stomach and slowly warm his blood. It truly was a better day for scotch than tea.

"She's always looked up to me." Ranford smiled with quiet affection. "And felicitations are in order for you as well, it appears." He lifted his brows. "Or perhaps condolences at the numbers of single misses who will forever ruin your peace at every social event henceforth until you wed."

Lucien laughed and shook his head. "This was not exactly the attention I intended to attract."

"Well, you did alter your appearance quite nicely." Ranford sipped his drink. "Truth be told, I thought you had an interest in Miss Bexley."

A knot twisted in Lucien's stomach. "I confess, she has been advising me on what to wear and do in the hope of being more appealing to the fairer sex."

"That was kind of her," Ranford replied. "She was exceptionally helpful with Julia's coming out last year. I couldn't have done it without her patient guidance."

The memory of Ranford dancing with Hannah rose forefront in Lucien's thoughts. As did Hannah's mention of helping the earl with Lady Julia's ball.

"I'm the woman men know will help when asked." Hannah's words resounded in Lucien's mind.

"Have you ever considered courting Miss Bexley?" Lucien asked.

Ranford held his glass between his two hands, staring for a long moment into its contents. "No," he answered slowly, and his gaze shifted to Lucien, his eyes narrowing somewhat. "Though my disinterest is through no fault of Miss Bexley."

Lucien remained quiet in an attempt to leave room for

Ranford to volunteer more information without being pressed.

"We have been friends long enough that I am surprised you have not noticed," Ranford replied.

"I appear to be rather daft when it comes to my interactions with others," Lucien answered ruefully, chagrined that the point was once more proven with a good friend.

Ranford chuckled. "Your head is always lodged in a book and turned up toward the sky in thought. Anyway, it is of no matter. It isn't something I generally mention to others. Only those I am closest to."

He glanced around, and Lucien realized he was about to be entrusted with a very guarded secret. Leaning forward in his seat, Lucien turned his ear toward his friend so Ranford would not need to speak loudly.

"I do not prefer the gentler sex in that manner," Ranford confessed. His brow furrowed with confirmation of Lucien's understanding.

After all Lucien's studies in Greek and Roman mythology, it was easy to precisely deduce what Ranford was getting at. Lucien nodded in understanding.

"But if I did…" Ranford tilted his head. "Miss Bexley would not have remained single past the end of last season. Though I know she declares her intention to remain unwed, I warrant others would see her as an agreeable potential wife. Maybe someone who will appeal to her as well."

"You mean I should leave her be so she can be pursued by others," Lucien summed up.

Ranford shrugged in apologetic confirmation.

"Her father said the same, and that is what I intend to do."

Lucien drank from the glass, a greater sip than he was used to and had to swallow hard to keep from sputtering.

"How do you feel about her?" Ranford asked suddenly.

Lucien did cough then. "Well, it doesn't seem to matter when the lady is uninterested in me. I'm afraid any chance I might have had with her, I've thoroughly botched."

Ranford tapped a finger on his glass. "I disagree. I've seen how she watches you."

Lucien shook his head. "I assure you she wants nothing to do with me."

His friend grinned at him. "Perhaps we will sit back and see how fate plays your hand. In the meantime, come to Vauxhall with me this Thursday. Madame Saqui is supposed to perform. I've had the pleasure of watching her tightrope dance once before, and she is exquisite."

"We'll be swarmed with debutantes," Lucien warned his friend. "And I have it on good authority my mother will also be in attendance."

Ranford smiled. "And I assure you, we will sit in a separate box than Lady Brightstone, affording you privacy for bride hunting."

It would do Lucien some good to get Hannah out of his thoughts. His numerous missteps with her were well beyond salvageable. First the kiss, then the poorly timed request to allow her to court him. Surely, she was not the only woman in all of London who could fascinate him with her open conversation and quick wit.

Lucien nodded. "Thursday it is."

Ranford tapped his glass with Lucien's, and the plan was formally made.

12

Vauxhall was an experience not to be missed. Hannah dined on paper-thin ham, watched the heart-stopping performance of Madame Saqui precariously teetering on a nearly invisible wire and thrilled at the array of colored lights as the garden lit up like magic.

"I'd like to propose a toast." Hannah held up a glass of wine, its warmth flowing pleasantly through her veins on the chilly evening.

Her friends lifted their glasses and turned their attention toward her.

"To our friendship," Hannah concluded.

The women all clinked their delicate stemware together and drank.

"I'm curious," Hannah said as though musing an idea that had suddenly come to her. "How do you all feel about the vow we made back at Lady Finch's?"

"The one to never wed?" Lucy asked with a smirk. "Suits me well enough. I'm not the marrying sort."

"It would be a relief to be free so long as my father would

allow it." Jillian sighed heavily. "Which I do not see being possible. But if I can manage, the pact still holds fast for me."

"I haven't thought of our vow in years." Elizabeth frowned slightly. "I'm not sure. I confess that the idea of a manor in the country has always been appealing, but also..."

"Romance," Lucy sighed dramatically.

They all laughed good-naturedly, and Elizabeth flushed a delicate shade of pink.

"One never knows when a gentleman might sweep a lady off her feet," Elizabeth protested.

"It isn't so much a husband necessarily that I want, or even love, but children..." Amy smiled softly.

"You can't have one without the other," Hannah said lightly.

Lucy stuck her finger in the air. "Well..."

"Lucy," Amy gasped as she swiftly looked about to ensure no one had overheard, and they all laughed again.

But even as Hannah joined in their shared mirth, there was a tug of disappointment in her friends' responses regarding the pact. She had put far too much stake into the simple agreement.

Amy was right. They had been practically girls when they signed it, with no idea who they were then or what life would bring their way.

While Hannah's prediction had been correct about her own future, her friends might fare far differently than what they anticipated when they signed the book. At this point, she might very well become a spinster in a large country manor all by herself.

The thought was not pleasant.

A clatter of commotion came from the right side of the

stage, where several women shifted through the crowd toward a gentleman. Hannah's stomach sank. Not just any gentleman…Lord Brightstone.

He was regal in a navy wool jacket with gold buttons and long tails, set nicely with a pair of buckskin breeches that admittedly hugged his finely sculpted legs in all the right places. His top hat was perched perfectly over freshly cut blond waves, and he fished something from the pocket of his light blue waistcoat.

Ah, yes, a pocket watch.

He had followed her suggestions and was successful because of it.

No, that was unfair, she had to admit grudgingly. He wasn't simply successful for having listened to a bit of fashion advice. He was successful because he wore those clothes so bloody well. His looser garments before did nothing to show off the expanse of his broad shoulders or the neatness of his waist and narrow hips.

He truly was a handsome man.

Now every woman in London knew it. She'd heard what they said about him, what was written in the scandal sheets. How he listened to women in a world where men talked over them, that he was a great conversationalist who always knew how to unlock a woman's deepest secrets.

That last bit had Hannah snorting at breakfast that morning and earned her a sharp look from her mother. But truly, the only thing he did to "unlock a woman's deepest secrets" was to use Hannah's suggestion of asking the questions and letting the woman fill in the gaps of silence while they danced. She'd heard enough women speaking of their time on the dance floor with him to know how often he implemented her recommendations.

But those women didn't see beyond the clothes or the title and wealth to the shy man she knew. They didn't appreciate how he could gaze up at the sky and know the stars and each story behind them.

They didn't deserve him.

"Hannah, do you want to leave?" Amy asked softly.

"I think…" Hannah's face burned at having been caught staring at Lucien. No, not Lucien - Lord Brightstone. "I think I should like to go to the retiring room."

"I'll join you." Elizabeth pushed to her feet, and together, the two of them slipped from the private box.

After a moment alone and a bit of cool water on her cheeks, Hannah was feeling markedly improved.

"We can stay here a moment longer if you prefer," Elizabeth said gently.

Hannah shook her head.

Elizabeth cast her a concerned glance. "We've already seen Madame Saqui perform. There is no reason for us to stay."

"Aside from the fireworks, you mean." Hannah waved off the implied suggestion that they should depart. Everyone knew the best part of Vauxhall was the fireworks. "It's been a delightful time, and I'm not at all inclined to depart early."

Elizabeth acquiesced with hesitation and strode out into the night once more toward the narrow hall that would lead them to her father's supper box. As she rounded a corner, she gave a slight gasp and deftly slid out of the way, inadvertently allowing Hannah to career into the person Elizabeth had narrowly avoided.

"Forgive me," a familiar voice said as Hannah staggered back. "Are you hurt, Miss Bexley?"

She gazed up at Lord Brightstone. His face was so shadowed, she couldn't see the shade of his eyes, though she knew them to be the most beautiful blue she'd ever become lost in. Of all the awful luck.

"I'm fine." Her voice was soft, breathy. All the more embarrassing, and she wished she could have a second chance to redo the moment.

"I wondered if you were free for a few minutes to speak?" he asked abruptly.

Hannah glanced to the retiring room behind her. "Were you following me?"

His eyes went wide. "No. No, this was a mere coincidence. A happy one."

"It looks like a nice evening for a walk," Elizabeth said cheerfully.

The evening was about as nice for taking a stroll as the tundra was for a ballroom.

Elizabeth shrugged as if realizing her suggestion was preposterous.

"Please," Lucien said. "I wish to explain myself, as I failed to do in our previous discussion."

Hannah bit her lip. Wasn't it better to cast him from her thoughts, from her heart?

Or was meeting with him giving her a chance for a different life? One where she didn't have to hang onto the hope that her friends would end up spinsters, especially when the likelihood was so slim.

Would she deprive Elizabeth of a chance at living her own romance? Or keep Amy from having the children she craved? Or Lucy the chance for a partner who might settle her wild manner? And poor Jillian didn't seem to have a choice in the matter, especially if her father had his way.

Perhaps it was for all those reasons that Hannah nodded. "Yes, I would like that."

"I'll fetch your wrap," Elizabeth said quickly, dashing off before Hannah could stop her.

In the second that it took her to retrieve the heavy wrap, Hannah and Lucien were entirely alone. Lucien. Because with him standing before her, tall and handsome and so achingly familiar, it was impossible to think of him so formally as Lord Brightstone.

"Thank you for agreeing to walk with me," he said in that thoughtful, quiet voice of his. It soothed a part of her she hadn't realized needed quieting until it was done.

There were many attributes about Lucien that appealed to her, and in these last few days of their distance, she had missed every one.

Elizabeth practically ran toward them, no doubt worried Hannah would change her mind if too much time passed, and almost threw the wrap around Hannah's shoulders.

"Take your time." Elizabeth grinned at them and waved.

Hannah tossed her an incredulous look, to which Elizabeth merely giggled in reply before leaving them alone once more. Lucien offered her his arm, which she accepted. The superfine wool was smooth beneath her gloved hand, his warmth evident and comforting.

The wind hit them like ice outside, but they both ignored its wrath and strolled as though the sun were dappling a spring garden before them. Even still, the frigid air was not enough to dampen the distinct scent of whale oil used to light the various colored lamps.

"I care for you, Hannah," Lucien said. "Incredibly so. I've missed your presence these last few days."

Well. She hadn't expected that. Doubt crept over her like armor.

Was the compliment simply part of his need to make up for what he told her about her father? Or—worse still—the humiliating confession she'd thrown spitefully at him?

"You needn't flatter me," she said rigidly.

"But it's true." He stopped and turned to her, his face partially illuminated by a green lantern nearby.

Her heart caught in her chest, locked there by a fledgling whisper of hope.

She gazed up at him, and a gust of wind blasted at them. An involuntary shiver rippled through her. Lucien put his arm around her shoulders and guided her into a darkened alcove where the wind could not touch them. His familiar scent was replaced with an expensive spice.

"You smell different," she observed.

He gave an embarrassed chuckle. "My valet suggested it. I actually dislike the scent."

"It isn't unpleasant," she replied. "But I prefer the way you smelled before."

They were close to one another in the limited space of the alcove so that the toes of her slippers touched those of his polished Hessians. Their eyes met, and the breath fled Hannah's lungs.

She knew that look on Lucien's face, the softening of his eyes as his stare swept down her face to her lips.

He was going to kiss her.

And she was going to let him.

THERE WAS SO much Lucien wished to say to Hannah. It hadn't truly been his intent to lure her to an alcove and kiss her.

Except that the inclement weather forced them into such tight quarters, and with her so close, her sweet citrus fragrance and her beauty beckoning him...he could not help himself. Especially not when he had spent every night since that kiss reliving the moment—the taste of her lips, the heat of her mouth, the fire that crackled inside him and tightened his loins.

"I haven't been able to stop thinking of you," he said raggedly.

She swallowed. "Nor I, you." Her breath came in a shaky exhale, and her lashes fluttered as she angled her face up.

"I kissed you before, and you did not want it," he said. "I will not do so again unless you wish me to."

Her teeth sank into that lower lip he wanted so desperately to suck into his mouth. She looked up at him. "I want you to kiss me."

Sweeter words had never been heard by any man.

He reached for her, caressing the line of her jaw with his gloved hand. It wasn't enough. With a growl, he withdrew his hand, wrenched off the glove and let his bare fingers caress her skin. She was softer than he imagined, like a rose petal, warm and tempting.

"Hannah," he whispered.

"Lucien."

He closed his eyes with pleasure at hearing his name breathy and eager on her lips. Without allowing himself to think—only to *feel* instead—he lowered his head and touched his mouth to hers.

Where last time she had tasted of lemonade and brandy, now she held the heady richness of wine. His hand shifted behind her head, cradling the weight of her luxurious hair against his palm as he deepened the kiss.

This time, she did not hesitate to part her lips, welcoming the brush of his tongue against hers with a little moan that left him thickening with need. Her tongue stroked his, tentatively at first and then with a need that matched his own.

Her hand lifted to his face, cold and absent gloves as well, running down the length of his neck to curl around toward the back. Desire pulsed white-hot, making him lose all sense of time. All sense of place.

There was no Vauxhall Gardens or an alcove where they might easily be seen. There was only him and Hannah and the attraction burning with an intensity neither could ignore.

She pushed against him, her curves evident through even her wrap. He trailed his hands over her, tracing the exquisite shape of her body. His cock ached as she arched toward him, straining toward her.

Her gasp whispered through their parted lips, and he knew she felt the force of his erection.

"Forgive me," he murmured. "I..."

But she arched her hips against the length of him. The pleasure of that slight pressure gripped him, making him swallow a groan to remain as quiet as possible. But he didn't want to quell the sounds of his desire. He wanted to growl and groan and snarl with a fervor he had never known.

He wanted this woman more than he wanted air to breathe.

Her mouth slanted over his in her mutual desire, little whimpers of enjoyment humming in the back of her throat. He kissed a path down the line of her jaw to her neck where her perfumed skin was sweet and sensual and more temptation than he could bear.

Hannah leaned her head back, giving him access as he nipped and kissed the graceful column of her throat and the delicate lobe of her ear. Her bosom was thrust toward him, and he could not stop his fingers from trailing down her neck to the edge of her bodice. A delightful exhale slipped from her lips, and he ran his fingertip along the creaminess of her skin there.

He wanted to draw the bodice down, to free her of her corset and cup her naked breasts in his hands. Instead, he skimmed down the front of her gown to where the hard point of her nipple stood against the thick fabric and lightly thumbed over it.

Her hands gripped his coat, holding onto him as he kissed away her moans.

The bud beneath his finger was so hard, so pert, he desperately longed to feel it beneath his touch. He shifted to block her entirely from view as he eased a hand into her bodice.

Hannah did not stop him but instead arched her chest toward him. His fingertips met her hot skin and found what he sought, playing over the nub adroitly as she closed her eyes with a sigh.

All he wanted was her pleasure. So it was without any

thought but to her needs that he lifted the length of her skirt higher. He watched her as he did so, drowning in a sea of deep, beautiful blue until his fingers met her smooth inner thighs, and she sucked in a surprised breath.

"I want to bring you pleasure," he softly murmured. "Your innocence will remain intact. You have my word." His fingertips danced over her inner thigh, teasing bit by bit higher toward the apex of her legs, an area he would not touch without her permission.

She nodded and licked her lips, so they glistened in the moonlight. "Please. I'm so…"

His fingertips brushed her sex, and she gasped sharply. She was hot and wet beneath his hand. If he had her in his bed, if she were his wife, it would be so easy to plunge into her and sate his desires.

But she was not his wife. She was an innocent.

He reminded himself of this as he traced her slit with his finger before brushing the sensitive bud at the top of her sex.

Her mouth opened in a silent cry, her eyes closing against the force of her pleasure. Lucien kissed her, drinking in her moans as his fingers learned her most intimate parts. The squeeze of her thighs tightened around his hand, and a low tremble quivered at her muscles.

She was close.

He picked up his pace, moving his finger faster over her. A firework popped in the distance and illuminated the sky with a fiery gold glow. Hannah whimpered.

Several cracks and booms lit up their world in an array of colors and brilliance as her sex spasmed with the telltale sign of her release. She clung to him with fisted hands and shuddered an exhale before finally opening her eyes to gaze up at him.

The fireworks continued to play over the world around them. "That was the most exquisite thing I've ever experienced," she whispered.

"It was for me too." And it was. He would recall that moment when the light of the fireworks danced over her face as her expression became one of pure bliss during her climax.

Somewhere in the distance came a shout, followed by laughter as some chaps in their cups reveled in the chilly night. Though far away, it was a reminder that they were not alone. They were not as private as he would like them to be. Someone might see.

Good God, what had he done?

He pulled his hand from beneath her skirt and withdrew the other from her bodice. His breath came in great fogging gasps in the icy air.

The spell was broken.

What had he done?

He had taken advantage of her and pushed the kiss further than it ever should have gone. Her lips were reddened with the force of his kisses, and her eyes bright with passion. Though her hair and gown were still in place, thankfully, she looked thoroughly loved.

And in public, no less.

"Hannah." His voice was a deep rumble, thick with desire. "I shouldn't...of all places...I..."

She shook her head. "Don't." She licked her lips. "Don't you dare say you regret this."

"You are better than this." He fisted a hand at his side, furious with himself, with his lack of control.

He had always been so in charge of his person. Never had he bent to his need in such a way.

But then, never had he been so tempted by a woman as he was with Miss Hannah Bexley.

His behavior had been reprehensible, especially with a lady like Hannah, who was good and pure and kind.

"Marry me," he said abruptly. It was a clunky, poorly thought-out proposal, but he could not forgive himself the liberties he had taken with her and not offer marriage.

She gaped at him. "I beg your pardon?"

"The way I've behaved, it was reprehensible. I'm asking for your hand to preserve your honor." Even as the words left his mouth, he knew they weren't what he wanted to say.

"Preserve my honor?" She frowned, and his stomach sank. "That's why you would wed me?"

"I'm a gentleman, and you're a lady," he replied. "I would never take advantage—"

"You didn't take advantage." Hurt replaced the desire in her eyes, glimmering with unshed tears. "I wanted…I wanted to kiss you. I wanted you to…to…do what you did…"

He had thoroughly ruined this. Again.

Damn his inability to articulate his thoughts better. But for some reason, the more something meant to him, the harder it was to compose it all into words.

"I want this," he said vehemently. "Us. Please, marry me."

She stared at him as if he'd asked her to cut off her hand. "No."

With that, she darted past him from the alcove and into the dark night.

"Hannah—wait." Lucien ran to follow her when a woman stepped in front of him in the middle of the path.

Lady Alison, the woman who had put herself at Lucien's side for the better part of the evening, curled a finger around a lock of her blonde hair. And the smile on her lips said she'd overheard everything.

13

There were very few times in Hannah's life that she allowed herself the luxury of imagining what it would be like to receive a proposal from a man. But in all those instances, never once had the reason been to "preserve her honor" after a heated kiss.

Well, more than a kiss.

Her knees were still soft with the force of…whatever that was. God, but it had been heavenly. Wicked and sinful and so absolutely amazing.

Never had she realized her body could experience sensations like that. How a simple finger could so expertly draw out such euphoria.

She hadn't thought the fireworks at Vauxhall Gardens could be improved upon. It appeared she was mistaken.

Admittedly, she had allowed too much. There were so many times she could have stopped him. He had even given her the choice, and she had asked for it. An unwanted shiver of pleasure teased down her back at the very memory. It all had been very pleasurable. Perhaps too much so.

As she strode quickly down the lantern-lit path, even the frigid night air could not quell the blaze of longing that lingered between her thighs and burned at her cheeks. If he had not stopped, how far might she have allowed him to go?

She had lost herself in the fantasy of Lucien, of what it would be like to free herself to be with him. Without fear of rejection, without cataloging the many ways that he might find her wanting. All of it had been cast aside to spread her wings and soar into the possibility of love.

At the end of it all, she liked Lucien for who he was before the veneer of fashion made him shine. And she would want him to like her in the same regard. Not for having shared such intimate indiscretions or for fear of her father's retribution.

But truly, as a man who would love her for who she was when she was nobody special at all.

Her eyes were hot with unshed tears.

Whatever love might be, it was more complicated than the effort was worth. This constant play of trust and hurt with Lucien was nothing she wanted to go through again. She had been right to try to shove him off to another lady and let her life fall into its usual lull. To some, such a world might be dull, but for her, it was security in knowing what each day would bring.

"They came out together some time ago." A woman's sharp voice cut through Hannah's thoughts.

Was that Lady Arksford?

Hannah was in no mood to put on airs to endure the acerbic woman and huddled back into a shadowed alcove to keep from being seen.

"I hadn't realized my son would be here tonight." The

other voice was familiar as well. "But I'd thought it was going rather well this evening until he disappeared with *her*."

Hannah's heart constricted at the recognition of Lady Brightstone. Clearly talking about Hannah.

"I specifically told him to use her for practice," Lady Brightstone huffed indignantly.

To use her for practice.

The words froze away whatever residual warmth remained from her passionate kiss with Lucien.

"Not to pursue her for marital options," the countess haughtily continued. "Her father is only a baron, and she is… well…do I even need to elaborate?"

"No," Lady Arksford replied dryly. "You do not."

Hannah knew she should speak up, to defend herself against such ugly accusations. Instead, she put her hand over her mouth to stifle a sob.

Lady Brightstone heaved an irritated sigh. "It is so dreadfully cold out here. Whatever he does or says with her ends tonight. When he returns home, I'll insist he leave that creature alone and pursue a woman worthy of the Lambert name."

That creature.

Hannah squeezed her eyes shut, hating the heat of tears leaking silently down her cheeks. And while she knew now more than ever that she ought to stand up for herself against these horrendous women, she absolutely could not do so with a quivering voice and wet cheeks.

And so, she stayed in the alcove like a coward until their footsteps faded and their harsh criticisms only existed where they circled in her mind. Even then, she remained hidden from view as she reeled over what she had overheard.

Lucien had used her for practice. While she knew that he

had asked her advice and had implemented her guidance so perfectly that he gained more popularity than Hannah herself had ever known. But practice?

Rage simmered low in her belly. Because as much as she wanted to reject the idea from her thoughts, it made sense.

The way he'd danced with her before dancing with anyone else, how he'd used her to sharpen his wit with her banter, even in the way he had taken her outside now to kiss her, to touch her. He'd known she would decline that terrible proposal. What woman would not?

Or perhaps that was practice too?

Bile burned up her throat. She pressed her icy hands to her cheeks to cool them, her gloves somehow having disappeared through the spiral of events that had occurred in only several short minutes.

She wished she could snap her fingers in that instant and immediately be home. But first, she would have to face her friends. Better them than anyone else in the world, at least. Finally, she slinked from her hidden location and went to the retiring room to freshen up before forcing herself to re-join her friends.

"There she is," Lucy sang out joyfully.

Their smiling faces fell as soon as they laid eyes on Hannah. As much as she tried to conceal her pain, it was too stark to shield.

"It didn't go as you planned," Jillian said matter-of-factly.

Amy opened her arms to offer an embrace, but Hannah shook her head mutely. She was too fragile right now and feared such comfort would shatter her composure.

"I'll go find someone to summon the carriage." Elizabeth pushed up from her chair.

"I'll find someone to break his leg," Lucy muttered. "Bollocks to that. I'll do it myself."

Hannah gave a weak smile. None of them asked for details as they tried to sooth her hurts and distracted her from the agony of her pain.

As much as she had dreaded having to see her friends after such humiliation, she was now glad to have them at her side. It was through them that she would recover from such betrayal.

What she did know, however, was that she would never, ever trust Lord Brightstone again.

Lucien regarded Lady Alison warily.

"Good evening, Lord Brightstone," she said innocently. "I trust you are having a pleasant evening?" With a pointed look behind her at Hannah's retreating form, she turned back to him with a smirk. "Or interesting one, at least."

Her coy behavior rankled him. Already his nerves were scratched bare from the interaction with Hannah. The abrupt and harsh change from extreme passion to total self-loathing at his inability to convey emotions.

"What may I help you with, Lady Alison?"

"I wouldn't mind sharing a few moments in that alcove with you." She peered around him to the small space he'd huddled in with Hannah. "It sounded as if you two were experiencing quite the moment."

Lucien's body heated with shame at what he'd done. He should have been more aware—or, at the very least, in better control of himself.

"But Miss Hannah Bexley?" She gave a harsh bark of laughter, all pretense of her delicate giggles and blushes gone.

He took a step forward, his irritation turning to ire. "Miss Bexley is a fine lady and one I would be proud to be seen with."

"It appears she does not share your sentiment." Lady Alison lifted a hand and examined her fitted kidskin gloves indifferently. "I can't say I'm surprised. You may be an honorable gentleman, but she is no lady."

Lucien narrowed his eyes. "I don't approve of your insinuation."

"It's not an insinuation." She tilted her chin at an arrogant angle. "Did you know I went to Lady Finch's Finishing School with Miss Bexley?"

While this was not something he was aware of, Lucien remained quiet, refusing to feed into whatever claim she intended to lay at his feet.

"She has never been a lady, not in the truest sense," Lady Alison mused. "Don't you want to know what I do?"

"Who she was or what she did is not any of my concern." And he meant every damn word. He knew Hannah for who she was now. Whatever she had done in her past did not define the woman who had so dazzled him with her brilliance.

"Even if she doesn't marry you, you ought to know." Lady Alison shrugged her shoulders and then paused to pet the thick fur stole draped around her torso. "She's the lightskirt type."

The claim was ridiculous. Hannah struck him as anything but a roundheel. Yes, she expressed her joy in a manner more jubilant than most, and yes, she was amorous when she'd been in his embrace. But that did not make her a "lightskirt type," as Lady Alison stated so crudely.

"There was a bit of a sordid affair between her and the stablehand while at the school." Lady Alison covered her mouth with her hand in an exaggerated show of shock. "Surely, you should care about that. A stablehand..." She dropped her hand away and said the latter part with a look of distaste curling her full red lips.

"I do hate to disappoint you, but I truly do not care." He moved to walk past her, but she put a brazen hand on his chest, stopping him.

"It would be a shame if someone were to discover this little tryst between you." Lady Alison bit her bottom lip. "Considering how popular you are now, such gossip would spread like wildfire."

She stepped closer, bringing the cloying sweetness of her perfume with her. "Miss Bexley would be ruined."

"Why would you do that?"

"Because I don't like her." She drew an invisible pattern on the lapel of his coat. "But I very much like you."

An uneasy sensation tightened in his stomach.

"Or at least, I like your popularity," she said airily. "I want you to seek out my father for permission to court me."

Lucien lifted a brow, certain he had heard her incorrectly. "I beg your pardon?"

"I do not believe I mumbled or stammered in my request." Her lips peeled back into a vicious smile. "You heard me. I want you to go to my father to ask for permission to court me."

Lucien stared at her in horror.

"Oh, come now." She pouted at him in mockery. "You

needn't look at me like that. I don't expect you to marry me. Why would I want an earl when I could have a duke?" Rolling her eyes, she continued, "You only need to court me long enough for people to notice. Don't worry, it shan't consume too much of your season." She tossed a blonde sausage-roll curl of hair behind her shoulder with a flippant air. "Then I can cease being with you once I've garnered the attention I need."

Good God, she had calculated everything in her bid to stretch to the top. And it had only required the few short moments that she had witnessed the tryst between him and Hannah for her to compose it all so thoroughly.

Lady Alison was proof that true evil did exist. Only now, such poison came to Lucien in primped curls and wearing some poor woodland creature strung about her shoulders like a vicious prize.

"Don't look so glum." She reached out with her gloved hand and touched the underside of his chin, elevating his face. "There will be many ladies waiting to soothe your wounded heart. I assure you this will be advantageous for us both."

"And if I refuse?"

Her eyes darkened. "Then Miss Bexley will never have the opportunity to wed any man, and it will be entirely your fault."

He hissed out a slow exhale, hating being trapped in such a position. "I'll think on it."

"You have one minute." Lady Alison arched a curved brow. "I'm not a patient woman."

If he agreed now, it didn't mean he still couldn't go to Hannah and explain the situation. Perhaps if he could make her understand how very deep his feelings were, she would agree to marry him. In such an instance, her reputation would be salvaged, and none of the ugliness need come up again.

"Very well," he replied stiffly.

A saccharine smile adorned Lady Alison's lips. "I'm so pleased to hear you've been convinced to see reason. We should return together. For appearance's sake, of course."

He wanted to decline, to stalk away from her and find Hannah that instant.

She tilted her head at his silence. "I'm sure you meant to offer me your arm." Condescension dripped from her tone.

Lucien extended his elbow toward her. She held onto him with a possessive grip that made him immediately miss the delicate caressing manner in which Hannah had cradled her hand in the crook of his arm.

They returned to the pavilion, but he managed to keep Lady Alison from the line of sight of Lord Langston's supper box, where Lucien could see Hannah and her friends.

Thankfully, they left within the hour, and he could finally give in to Lady Alison's plaintive pouts to be in a position where they could be seen by all.

It was a horribly miserable night, and Lucien was only too glad to be released from Lady Alison's clutches to return home finally. However, upon entry into the house, his mother was waiting for him, a cup of tea at her side. No cream. No sugar. As strong and bitter as possible.

Like her.

She studied him with a shrewd demeanor as he entered. "Who were you with this evening?"

He sighed, weary from the night's events and in no mood for an interrogation. "Good evening, Mother. It's late, and I intend to retire."

She stiffened. "I did not wait up for you to be so readily brushed off. I know you were with that Bexley chit."

"Miss Bexley," he corrected.

"You are to stay far from her, do you understand?"

He shook his head. "I'm not a child to order about as you please. I happen to hold Miss Bexley in the highest esteem and refuse to stand by as you speak of her in so degrading a manner."

"Degrading?" Her head snapped back with obvious offense.

"Yes, degrading." He squared his shoulders and faced her. "The gossip is unseemly. I will choose a wife based on my discretion. It is a grandchild you want, and I will do all in my power to deliver it. But whomever the lady of my choosing is, she will be accepted by you or I will retire to the country this instant and delay marrying."

His threat hung in the air between them.

"You know your role, Lucien," Lady Brightstone said archly. "You must have an heir."

"And I'll fulfill my role," he replied. "But it does not mean I have to do it while you are still alive. I refuse to subject my wife to you, whoever she may be."

His mother sucked in a breath as if he had struck her, and it almost made him feel ashamed of his words. Almost.

She had shoved and bullied everyone in her path, forcing them to conform to her will. He was not such a pawn.

"Old men wed young wives and have children all the time," Lucien continued. "I have no qualms with waiting, but I do very much protest your belief that you have a say in the matter regarding who I will spend the rest of my life with."

"Well." She folded her arms over her narrow chest, blinking in surprise at the affront.

"I would also suggest you keep your strong opinions to yourself lest you find yourself weighed and judged. I wager you would not like the assessments."

Her mouth fell open. "Lucien," she hissed, appalled.

He stood in place, his stance wide, waiting for retaliation. Lady Brightstone pushed off the couch to her full height. In the candlelight, her face appeared wizened, lined with exhaustion that dulled her eyes. For the first time in Lucien's life, his mother appeared truly aged.

It softened the steel in his demeanor somewhat, but still, he held his ground. She always attacked when she sensed anything she perceived as weakness.

Instead, she gazed at him, her gray eyes assessing his for a long, quiet moment. Finally, she patted his cheek with more affection than she had ever shown him. "It appears there is some of me in you after all, my son." She nodded approvingly, then shifted to pass him. "Good evening, Lucien."

With that, she quit the room.

But his mother was only one hurdle to clear before he could wed Hannah. The other would be Hannah herself and the reparations he knew would be difficult to make.

THERE HAD BEEN little sleep for Hannah the night following Vauxhall Gardens. Lady Brightstone's words resounded in her head, mocking her.

And yet, every time Hannah closed her eyes, her thoughts drifted toward the memory of Lucien's mouth on hers, the exquisite way he had touched her. Her traitorous body heated with a desire that pulsed unsated in her veins.

Would he kiss other women as he had her? Would he tease his tongue over their throats and sweep the tips of his fingers between their thighs? Would he set them alight with a longing so great, they could not forget him no matter how hard they tried? No matter how undeserving of their time and their heart's energy he was.

After all, she had merely been practice for him.

It was crueler than she could accept. But still, she had heard the words herself.

That morning, she refused to allow Mary to draw the shades back, preferring the cool darkness of the room against her misery.

"My dearest Hannah, there is a visitor for you downstairs," Mary said excitedly.

Hannah rolled away from her maid, wanting only solitude to nurse the empty ache in her chest.

"It's Lord Brightstone," Mary chirped pleasantly.

Hannah could control the pain no longer, and a piteous cry wrenched from her heart. "I would sooner die than see him again," she said between gasping sobs.

Mary left at once and returned moments later with a damp cloth. "You needn't worry about him ever again," she soothed. "Lord Westwich is seeing to him at this very moment."

And, with that reassurance in mind, Hannah relinquished herself to Mary's coddling.

～

Time was a cruel mistress as it slowly dragged from one minute to the next, each seeming to last the span of an hour. Lucien's foot bounced anxiously against the Brussels weave carpet in the drawing room at Westwich Place. But with Hannah the night before, time had slipped through his fingers like sand, passing too quickly for him to relish it to the extent he longed to.

He only hoped he could convince her of his true intent, of the power of his feelings for her. The bit about Lady Alison could come later. After all, Hannah ought to know of the other woman's vitriol against her. But his failed attempts had taught him he needed to tell Hannah first why he longed to be with her.

That "why" was what would win her over now.

He had spent the night putting pen to paper, the way he expressed himself best. Once the enormity of his emotions had emptied from his jumbled mind into an orderly state on the page, the details were easier to assess, to remember, and would be recalled more readily for him to tell her.

Hannah would know exactly what she meant to him. If she felt for him even half of what he did for her, she would agree to marry him in an instant. Then, her reputation would be spared, he would not need to subject himself to a false courtship with Lady Alison and he and Hannah could begin their life together at once.

Everything would work out perfectly.

Except that when the door to the drawing room opened, it was not Hannah at all, but Lord Westwich. A very stern-faced Lord Westwich.

He strode into the room. "Lord Brightstone, I did not expect to see you back so soon." There was an edge to his civility, and it cut a swath through all pretenses of polite conversation. "Nor did I anticipate you would be so close to my daughter again."

"She is exactly the reason I'm here," Lucien replied.

Lord Westwich lowered his head, glaring at him. "She is exactly the reason you should leave."

Lucien frowned. Was she so very upset at him for his proposal after that kiss?

"I don't—"

"With all due respect, Lord Brightstone, you have harmed the person in this world I cherish above all others." A rattle came from the double doors. "In addition, of course, to my beloved wife," he said over his shoulder in the direction of the doors. "I should like for you to leave."

A protest lingered on the tip of Lucien's tongue. He could not yield when he so dearly cared for Hannah.

But even as he opened his mouth, Lord Westwich's rage melted away to sorrow, his large blue eyes so bright with hurt that it slammed Lucien in the chest.

"Please," Lord Westwich said softly in a pleading tone. "You've done enough hurt to my little girl."

And it was in that beseeching request Lucien saw exactly how deeply he had wounded Hannah this time. It was that stark understanding in the end that ultimately made him give up the fight.

14

Hannah was content to let the season pass her by. A fortnight faded away on the wings of time since the incident with Lord Brightstone. He had not returned to the house since her father met with him on her behalf.

She attended several soirees, of course, and a ball or two, but they lacked the brilliance and color and joy they once held. All she wanted now was a departure from the coldness of London for the embrace of nature and wilderness in their country estate. She longed for the balm of solitude and the stretch of freedom, far away from prying eyes and waspish tongues.

There had been only one time she'd seen Lord Brightstone at a soiree, and while his gaze fell on her and lingered, she ensured she did not once acknowledge his presence in the room. Her heart knew better, however, and beat in great, heavy thuds that remained with her not only through the night but for several interminable days after.

It was on an afternoon not long after that when Hannah

lay listless in her bed, her hand resting atop a novel she could not bring herself to finish, a knock came at the door.

Curious, she sat up.

Mary usually had a much louder knock to ensure she wasn't being ignored, as that had been a habit of Hannah's as a girl when she'd been too preoccupied with play to pay proper attention. The quiet knock sounded again, and then, without her answer, the knob turned.

Who would enter her room without permission?

A woman with dark hair and a sarcastic smirk on her lips peeked in, saw Hannah and grinned.

"Lucy?"

She laughed quietly and glided into the room. "I knew you'd be in here. The others are downstairs asking your poor butler for various odds and ends in an attempt to occupy him from seeing me come up here." Her mirth faded. "Why won't you see us?"

Hannah shook her head. "I'm so very unhappy," she confessed. "I know you all love me for my laughter and jests and how joyful I always am. To be so melancholy is too unappealing to make others endure. I could not subject you to that, not when I love you all so dearly."

"Oh, Hannah." Lucy sank onto the bed beside her and pushed a lank red curl back behind Hannah's ear. "We love you in all the ways we can get you, whether it's a smile we are sharing or a hurt we want to help soothe. Especially Amy—you do know that is what she lives for, to heal us all."

Hannah chuckled lightly. "She truly is so nurturing."

"It's one of the many reasons why we cherish her. And if she were suddenly unable to help us, would that make us care for her any less?" Lucy raised her eyebrows.

"No," Hannah immediately replied, almost offended by the notion. "Of course not."

Lucy held out her hands, palm up in demonstration. "And nor would we want to shun your company if you weren't happy. Come now, would I have dodged your butler to sneak up here if we weren't truly worried about you?"

Hannah threw her a skeptical look.

"Very well." Lucy sighed. "Perhaps, depending on the situation. But would Elizabeth have supported it? Or Amy, for that matter?"

"Fair point," Hannah grudgingly admitted.

Lucy took Hannah's arm and pulled gently. "Now, please join us downstairs before I have to add abduction to my list of crimes."

With that, Hannah allowed herself to be encouraged from the bed and led down to the drawing room, where poor Jones shook his head before the other women. "But we don't have blue silk umbrellas."

He started as Hannah and Lucy entered.

"Thank you, Jones," Hannah said to her frazzled butler. "I'm here now and can handle these hellions."

He cast a severe look at Lucy, who merely smiled sweetly at him in a quiet reply.

When he left, Hannah's friends rushed toward her, capturing her in the warmth of their embrace.

"Now, tell us what is amiss." Amy's soft brown eyes locked on Hannah's.

"And don't you dare say 'nothing,'" Lucy warned.

"Because we can see right through you," Jillian added.

Elizabeth curled her hand into Hannah's. The gesture was one of support when Hannah needed it most.

"I'm afraid it's a long story," she bemoaned.

"We have a fresh teapot and enough cakes to keep Jillian happy," Elizabeth said.

In response to this, Jillian leaned forward to capture the largest tea cake with the biggest dollop of frosting and nibbled it with a contented smile.

Hannah started at the beginning when she saw Lucien in the country, this time being entirely honest about their interaction and his appeal for her assistance in making him more fashionable.

"I knew it," Lucy hissed. "No man with Lord Brightstone's bookish ways immediately becomes a gentleman's fashion plate over the course of a few months."

"And why did he never consider you?" Elizabeth asked indignantly. "That would have been the ideal opportunity to inquire if you would allow yourself to be courted by him."

"I'm afraid I told him I had no interest in marriage." And so Hannah went on to confess how she truly had recalled their pact all those years ago at Lady Finch's and how much she had cherished it in the hopes of never having to be hurt by rejection and disappointment.

For all the good that had done.

"If I'm being entirely honest, I was rather looking forward to having a manor with all of us together in the country." Hannah smiled at her friends. "I could imagine Jillian working on her art, Elizabeth endlessly reading scores of books, Lucy filling the music room with the loveliest sounds, Amy baking decadent treats we would all enjoy." Hannah gave a wistful smile. "It seemed the perfect plan. And far better than the awfulness of dealing with suitors."

"Well, I'll concede that it would be far better than this

suitor business," Jillian announced, doubtless at her limit from her marital pursuits through the last few years.

"But that isn't all of it," Hannah said miserably and told them about the ill-fated kisses. Her face burned with humiliation as she admitted how he had asked her to court him after her father had words with him. Of course, she also shared the poorly timed marriage proposal after their impassioned kiss that led to a smidge more. She did not elaborate on the "smidge more" with the maids likely listening in on the conversation on behalf of Lady Westwich.

"And he never approached you again?" Elizabeth asked in horror.

"He tried, but I refused to see him," Hannah replied. "My father did instead, and I haven't seen Lord Brightstone since. Well, except for at Lady Whimbly's soirée, but we didn't speak. I doubt Lady Alison would ever allow him to, even if he were so inclined."

"But, Hannah," Elizabeth said gently. "You cannot close your heart to the possibility of love."

That familiar ache slammed into Hannah's chest, and tears sprang to her eyes once more. "And who would love me?"

"We do." Amy hugged her. "And if you open yourself to the possibility, I think you'll find there are others who would be honored to fall deeply in love with you."

Hannah drew in a pained breath. Her heart was still wounded, and the idea of placing it out there for someone else to step on was terrifying.

"Or you could set it all aside," Lucy suggested.

Amy tilted her head in chastisement. Lucy, of course, ignored her. "Don't think about love or men or Debrett's or any such nonsense because that's what it all is. Instead, think of how much you love dancing and seeing us at balls. Think of how much you love to dress up. And if nothing else, think about how much faster the season will go by with happiness rather than languishing about in your bed."

"Lucy makes a very good point." Jillian reached for Hannah's hand. "Shrug it all off and enjoy your time with us."

"That's when romance happens usually," Elizabeth added excitedly.

This time it was Lucy who shot the sharp, reproaching look.

But they were right. All of them, in their own ways. The days of lazing about in her bed made the season stretch on interminably, and it was only just beginning. There would still be months to endure.

It would be far more agreeable to don her finest dresses, sip lemonade with her closest friends and dance when the opportunity presented itself. The season would close in no time, and she would be free to return to the country once more.

She would live her life for herself and no one else.

A FAMILIAR LAUGH rose over the sound of the orchestra, unfettered and charmingly joyful. Lucien spun Lady Alison on the dance floor and glanced in that direction.

Hannah.

His heart constricted.

She wore a silver-and-blue gown that made her eyes look like sapphires, and glossy silver ribbons were wound through her hair. As usual, she was surrounded by her friends, her hand over her mouth in a poor attempt to squelch the laugh she hated so much. And that he simply adored.

He hadn't seen her since Lady Whimbly's soirée. She'd appeared so melancholic then, her smile nonexistent and her light dimmed. Seeing her thus, and knowing he had a part in her sorrow, had lodged in him like a stubborn thorn.

While he was pleased to see her happy again, her exuberance made him long with a visceral pang to be in her presence.

"Pay attention," Lady Alison hissed. "You almost went the wrong way."

He muttered his apology but struggled to draw his focus from Hannah.

Lady Alison followed the line of his focus. "It won't do to have you gaping at her like some starving puppy at a feast. You're supposed to be with me if you recall? Come, it's my favorite part of the dance, and the Duke of Dudley is watching."

"The Duke of Dudley is a step away from being engaged to Lady Jillian." Lucien caught Lady Alison by her waist and hoisted her into the air.

She struck a pose while elevated, her expression seraphic as if she truly was a sweet, innocent debutante. Lucien knew better.

When she landed, she frowned at him. "You could have held me up longer."

"Then we would have missed the next turn." He recalled now more than ever why dancing was so loathsome.

But Lady Alison giggled as if he'd said the wittiest thing and batted her eyes at him. "The duke is looking," she whispered. "Gaze at me with pure adoration."

"I'm afraid that is impossible," Lucien ground out.

Her hand squeezed his. "Try."

He sighed and stared down at her. She was lovely in the way ice was, glittering with beauty but cold and unyielding. Instead, he imagined she was Hannah, that he had the opportunity to dance with her, be near her, be privy to the fascinating insights and happiness that she always freely shared.

With that thought firmly lodged in his mind, he did what Lady Alison asked and studied her with complete adoration.

Her eyes widened and she blinked, her cheeks flushing pink. "Why, Lord Brightstone, if you were a duke, I should have my entire attention set on you simply for how you're looking at me."

The music slowed, and he bowed to her as she curtseyed. "In that case, I've never been so glad to be merely an earl," he replied, taking her hand to lead her back to the edges of the ballroom where an assortment of male suitors waited to claim her hand in a dance.

She scoffed but had to dull the sharpness of her tongue with so many witnesses around to prevent her beloved duke from overhearing. Not that he was as beloved as was his title and his wealth.

The duke approached Lady Alison first, casting aside the attention of a very disinterested Lady Jillian. As the duke swept Lady Alison onto the dance floor, Lucien searched the crowd, desperate for another glimpse of Hannah.

When he located her across the room, her face almost entirely visible with how she faced her friends, he knew he should look away. Except that she was so exquisite, with her cheeks rosy with good health and her eyes twinkling. She was animated as she spoke, her hands moving as she regaled a story that he wished he were close enough to overhear.

How he wished he could approach her now, to confess why he was with Lady Alison, that the arduous effort was all for her. And truly, it was.

Not only to protect her reputation from Lady Alison's threat to tell the ton of that night in Vauxhall Gardens but also to guard Hannah's heart against being hurt by him again.

The memory of Lord Westwich's agonized expression followed Lucien through every day, a warning never to cause Hannah such pain again.

Ranford appeared beside Lucien. "You should go to her."

"I'm courting Lady Alison," Lucien replied without feeling.

Ranford slid him a skeptical look. "And I'm finally going to be honest with the ton about who I'd truly like to wed."

"Ever the cynic," Lucien tsked.

"How are you not cynical after everything you've dealt with?" Ranford asked with a shake of his head.

"I'm doing it for her." Lucien didn't need to specify who "her" was. They both knew.

He had confessed the truth of it all to Ranford after Lucien and Lady Alison had first appeared in public together and the earl cornered him to ask if he'd gone entirely mad.

There were many days Lucien *did* feel like a Bedlamite for his decision. Especially in times such as this when Hannah was only a few dozen steps away—when the exquisite force of her presence reminded him of everything he had lost.

"Do excuse me. I'm in need of refreshment," Ranford said abruptly. In a lower, quieter voice, he added, "Your mother is approaching."

With that, Lucien's friend slipped into the crowd, abandoning Lucien to Lady Brightstone's gloating smirk.

"You have done very well, my son." She inhaled deeply as she settled beside him, the kind of breath one took when they had completed a difficult job. "Lady Alison will be an ideal addition to our household."

He had *not* confessed his situation to his mother. Doubtless, she would be heartbroken when Lady Alison finally ended Lucien's courtship for a wealthier man with a more noble title. For Lucien's part, he wished he knew when it might happen so that he could count down the days to his freedom.

"You should have care to mind the duke around your lady." His mother rested her hands firmly on the polished silver head of her cane. "He seems most interested."

Lucien could not have been more grateful for that interest but did not say as much aloud. His mother's focus wandered across the room to Hannah, and her mouth tightened. He tensed, waiting for a biting comment.

"You do not appear concerned about the duke," Lady Brightstone mused. "However, you do still seem to be very concerned about Miss Bexley."

Lucien cast a warning glance at his mother and found she watched him carefully with concern lining the thin skin on her forehead. "It's her you want, isn't it?" she asked.

The curious manner in which she studied him almost appeared to be affection.

"It doesn't matter," Lucien replied in a stiff tone. "There will be no further opportunities to pursue something with Miss Bexley. I'm sure that delights you to no end."

She frowned. "I don't wish to see you unhappy. I only want

what is best for you. But what I thought you needed, who I thought you were…I was wrong." Her attention shifted back to Hannah once more, her displeasure carving fresh lines onto either side of her mouth. "I have made egregious mistakes."

Something was not right with Lady Brightstone. Her demeanor had been altered for the last few weeks since the night he defended himself against her. She had been distant, quiet, almost demure. But never before had she acted in such a manner as she did now, nor had she ever admitted to being wrong before. About anything. To anyone.

"Shall I fetch the physician?" Lucien asked hesitantly.

His mother touched his forearm. "You opened the door for me to look at myself, Lucien. And I did not like what I saw. I have been petty and sharp and impossible. When your older brother passed…" She shook her head, still unable to talk about the brother that had died before Lucien was born, an unknown boy to Lucien that he was forbidden from ever mentioning. "I thought if I kept everyone far away, I couldn't hurt anymore. I did not think of who I might hurt instead."

She patted his sleeve. "If Miss Bexley is who you want, then you should go to her."

Lucien put his hand over his mother's, appreciating the note of affection. "Thank you." He couldn't stop the sigh that followed. "But I am afraid it's far too late."

15

There were few things in life more enjoyable than friendship. Once Hannah allowed herself to shrug off the overbearing cape of sorrow, she sincerely did have a grand time during the season.

Despite Elizabeth's romantic notions that love would seek out Hannah once she stopped looking, it was Lucy's advice that rang truest of all. Hannah put her focus on spending time with the other ladies, donning her finest gowns and dancing when asked without any expectation for what— or whom— the next waltz may bring.

Though Lucien was also at the social events she attended, she ignored him entirely, and even his very presence with Lady Alison did not trouble her a whit. Or so she liked to tell herself. There were many times in the evenings after the candle by her bed had been snuffed, and she was left in the dark with her thoughts, that she relived the passionate moments they'd shared. Those lonely hours were when the ache of missing him was most poignant.

Lucien was a sore spot in her soul that never seemed to heal.

Fortunately, no one saw that part of her she managed to mask so well.

At least, no one but Mary, who continued to maintain the furrow of worry at her brow whenever she studied Hannah too long. Which was why it was extraordinarily strange that on the morning of Lady Gentry's ball, as Mary was putting Hannah's hair up, that she would broach the topic of Lucien.

"I have a friend who is in the employ of Lambert Abbey," she began.

Hannah immediately stiffened, every muscle locking into place with the need to gird herself from the impact of whatever Mary meant to say.

"Evidently, your Lord Brightstone is exceedingly unhappy." Mary eased a pin into Hannah's hair.

Hannah tried to push this thought from her mind. "His contentment is not my concern." A knot of tension formed at the back of her neck. She hated the gossip about him and had heard plenty in the last few weeks regarding not only Lucien but also Lady Alison. Hannah could stand no more.

Mary twisted another lock of hair, securing it back against the others with a pin. "But as it happens, the reason he—"

"Mary, please." There was a tremble to Hannah's voice that stilled Mary's efforts.

"I thought I might have news that could..." Mary's voice trailed off.

"There is nothing that anyone can say that would explain away the idea of my being used as practice for him." Hannah lifted her chin, finding solace in her newfound strength to set

Lucien aside. "If he is unhappy, he has made his decisions, and I ask you to please stop discussing him."

Mary lowered her gaze. "Yes, my lady."

She did not mention him again as the day wore on, nor when she readied Hannah for the ball that evening. But it did not mean that Hannah had stopped thinking of Lucien. The very mention of his name lodged him in her mind like a stubborn stain that could never be fully removed.

Her friends were all in attendance at the evening's ball, which immediately elevated her mood. But so were Lucien and Lady Alison, which decidedly dropped her mood once more.

"I heard some interesting news about Lord Brightstone today," Elizabeth began once they were all gathered around.

"Oh, do tell," Lucy demanded eagerly.

"I don't care to hear it," Hannah said as politely as possible.

Amy nudged her. "Aren't you the least bit curious?"

Hannah was not. How could she be when the very mention of his name was like a fresh slice to her wounded heart?

"By all means, please proceed." Hannah waved a hand at them to continue. "I'll help myself to a bit of lemonade."

Lady Gentry had something of a sweet tooth, and so it was that the lemonade at all her social functions was some of the best in London.

Hannah's friends all shared a look.

"Come now," Hannah protested at their disappointment. "I'm a grown woman and perfectly capable of securing a glass of lemonade on my own." She winked at Elizabeth. "Perhaps love will find me as I do."

"I'll join you," Jillian said as she gave a subtle nod in Lucy's direction.

That nod was the first indication something was amiss. Something Hannah was not privy to.

Before she could protest, Jillian curled her hand around the crook of Hannah's elbow and led her away. "Let's leave them to their gossip."

As they made their way through the crowded ballroom, the dancing couples swept by in circles over the center of the dance floor. One pair in particular caught both Hannah and Jillian's attention as they twirled past. The Duke of Dudley and Lady Alison, both engrossed in their conversation.

Jillian watched them with a little smile pulling at her lips. "It's such a relief to see those two together."

"I imagine you're glad for the reprieve from his company," Hannah replied.

Since the duke had been spending more time with Lady Alison, he was seldom around Jillian. Without his oppressive person looming over her, Jillian laughed again and shared her wondrously unique ideas and thoughts. It was as though he had blocked the sunlight from her world, and she shone without him once more.

"Even more than that..." Jillian took a glass of lemonade. "It frees up Lord Brightstone for you."

It was as unexpected as Mary's comment had been earlier that day. There was something amiss with Hannah's friends. But what?

"You must come quickly." Lucy was suddenly at Hannah's side, grabbing her arm and pulling her.

Hannah did not resist, allowing herself to be dragged from

the lemonade table before she could even pour a glass. "What is it?" She asked, alarmed.

Lucy's hand was like ice. "A cat…"

Hannah was immediately listening. "What of it?"

"I think it fell into the pond outside." Lucy tugged her toward the terrace. "I saw it through the window. It was perched on the edge as cats do, you know. Then, it just fell in."

"It just fell in?" Hannah shook her head. "Did it stumble or slip?"

"No, it…" Lucy held her hand upright, then dropped it to the right and made a small splashing sound.

"How unusual, the poor dear." Hannah's heart clenched at the awfulness of such a thing. "Did it scamper out?"

Lucy hesitated as if she did not understand the question, then quickly said, "No. No, it did not."

"Oh, there must be something horribly wrong with it." Hannah was the one encouraging Lucy to go faster now. "It's so cold outside that the thing will likely freeze. Why didn't you save it?"

"I don't know anything about the little beasts but am aware of your fondness for them." Lucy exited through the terrace door.

Hannah rushed outside and immediately spotted the pond several steps from the terrace. They raced down the short flight of stairs into the garden and through the moonlit path to the pool of water.

The surface was so still that it perfectly reflected the moon like a mirror.

"Where is it?" Hannah shook her head.

"It has to be here somewhere," Lucy said, somewhat bewildered.

But in looking at the surrounding area of the pond, Hannah realized there were no darkened areas suggesting drops of water. Hannah looked at Lucy in shock, thoroughly confused.

There was no cat.

So, why had she been led out into the garden on such a bitterly cold night?

THE RESPITE from Lady Alison while she danced with the duke was one Lucien wished might last forever. His only regret was that during his conversation with his mother, he had lost sight of Hannah.

As the music ended, the muscles along the back of his neck tensed in anticipation of having to entertain Lady Alison once more. In the last few interactions, he had become less and less patient with her petulant and cruel behavior. She had already entwined herself around the duke like an invasive weed. Why did she need to keep her grip on Lucien as well?

A curious thing happened as Lady Alison neared. Lady Jillian and Lady Elizabeth approached her out of nowhere, barring her way toward him.

He would have to thank them later for their intervention, which would afford him a few more moments of blissful silence.

"Lord Brightstone."

He turned to the sound of the gentle voice and found Miss Honeyfield gazing sweetly at him. "If you had the opportunity to speak to Miss Bexley again, to explain your side of the situation, would you spare a moment?"

"I have a lifetime of moments to spare if she would accept them," he answered.

Miss Honeyfield beamed. "I hoped you might say something of the sort. She's on the terrace."

He did not bother looking back at Lady Alison. If given the opportunity to be with Hannah, he would never once regret turning his back on the loathsome woman who had sucked the life from his soul that past fortnight.

Ladies planted themselves opportunistically in his path, but he darted around them, not caring if his actions were unseemly. He was determined to reach the terrace as swiftly as was possible. When he finally pushed outside, he discovered Hannah on her hands and knees, peering out into the garden.

The scene was admittedly a strange one, and it gave him pause. At least, until Miss Beauchamp wished him luck, swept past him and closed the door behind her. He did not miss the distinct click of the lock sliding into place.

Hannah straightened, locked eyes with him and froze. "Are you looking for the cat as well?" she asked with hesitation, sensing something was amiss. "I confess, I don't think there is one, despite Lucy's insistence that it's out here." She scanned the area. "Where is Lucy?"

"She left." He gestured to the door.

Hannah frowned. "And why are you here?"

"I was instructed to come out here to speak with you if I so desired, to present my side of what has transpired between us." He stepped closer but stopped his advancement when she tensed.

"Who would say that?" she asked.

"Miss Honeyfield," he replied. "I believe this was a scheme you were not privy to." Disappointment crushed at his chest.

"I was not." Her chin lifted with indignation. "I don't even have my cloak…" The words died on her tongue as she peered at something behind Lucien.

He turned to see a bundle of cloth set upon a table beside the door. Her cloak, apparently. He took the item and brought it to her, spreading it over her shoulders.

"I realize now this was not your idea," he said. "But I should still appreciate the opportunity to speak to you."

A rattle sounded at the door as someone tried to open it.

Hannah glanced in the direction of the locked door and sighed. "It doesn't appear I have much of a choice."

"No, it does not." Though Lucien spoke grimly, he had never been so overjoyed at a scheme in his life. "And I'm glad for it."

Hannah blinked up at him.

He gently grasped her hand. "I've wanted this moment since I botched my proposal to you. I don't always know the right way to articulate how I'm feeling. Indeed, I have a terrible habit of saying things entirely wrong. The way I have with you."

She regarded their joined hands but did not withdraw from his grip.

"The truth of the matter is…" He thought back to the letter he'd written to her, where his heart poured out like poetry onto the page. "The truth is that I believe I'm in love with you."

Hannah's eyes flew up to meet his. "I beg your pardon?"

"No." He shook his head and her brows furrowed. "No, I *know* I'm in love with you," he said vehemently.

"Love?" the word squeaked from her mouth as her eyes went wide.

"I haven't stopped thinking of you for a single moment since you fell into my life." The corner of his lip twitched. "Quite literally."

Her mouth lifted in a slight smile.

"It was your vivacity," he quickly said before he could ruin it all over again. "The openness of your nature, the way you forged your path and strode onward in your carefree manner. It's the way you laugh, the way you so brilliantly experience and share your joy." He closed the distance between them and reached out to stroke her face with the back of his gloved hand. "You are *radiant*, Hannah."

She pulled away from him. "Is this practice?"

"What do you mean?" he asked, momentarily taken aback.

While there had been difficulties between them, he'd assumed she would be glad of his confession. That there might be a possibility for her to give him a chance to reclaim her heart as she had his.

"If it is practice, you needn't bother." Her voice wavered, and her eyes shone with tears. "Because you're terribly good at it."

He frowned. "Practice?"

"I overheard your mother say that you were using me for practice, not to pursue for marital options." Hannah balled her hands into fists and straightened her back. "You needn't bother as you have far surpassed your tutor."

"My mother made that heinous suggestion once, and at that time, I not only declined her cruel idea but I also defended your character. You are a good person. I have always known that."

"And yet the likes of Lady Alison managed to secure your affections so quickly," Hannah said bitterly.

"I did that for you." Lucien's pulse sped up. This was exactly why he needed a private moment to speak with Hannah. Not only inclined to confess his love but also to explain Lady Alison. She had slipped so far from his mind when he first saw Hannah that he'd nearly forgotten.

"She saw us that night," he explained.

Hannah's cheeks went red. "Which night?"

"At Vauxhall Gardens."

A horrified moan escaped her throat, and she covered her face with her hands.

"Lady Alison threatened to spread the word around the ton about our tryst," he said. "Unless I courted her long enough to encourage the attention of wealthier suitors."

Hannah dropped her hands and stared at him incredulously.

"I tried to go to you," he continued. "To tell you, to ask you to marry me to protect you from the salacious gossips."

"But I refused to see you," Hannah concluded. "I'm sure it's been terrible for you with Lady Alison."

He sighed. "Absolutely awful."

"I'm well aware. I went to finishing school with her."

"I know." Lucien scoffed. "She said—"

Hannah tilted her head for him to go on. When he did not, she lifted her brow. "What did she say?"

"Nothing I cared about. Nothing that would have kept me from you."

"What did she say?" Hannah asked, more insistently this time.

Lucien grimaced at having to voice Lady Alison's ugly

words aloud. "That there had been a dalliance...with the stablehand."

"Me?" Hannah asked.

Lucien nodded. "But I don't care. Hannah, that was your past and anything you'd done—"

Hannah started laughing. Not in the cruel way Lady Alison often did, but in that pure, open tinkling laugh Hannah gave when she was genuinely amused.

"That was her," Hannah said between breathless giggles. "Lady Alison was the one who had the tryst with the stablehand. I should know because I'm the one who interrupted their...interlude."

Suddenly, Lucien felt foolish for having ever believed Lady Alison's claim in the first place. "I thought I was protecting you."

"You endured Lady Alison for a fortnight for me? Even after I refused you. Even after my father advised you to never speak to me again."

Lucien nodded.

"Why would you do that?" she whispered.

"I told you," he said, his voice hoarse with emotion. "I love you."

Her head tilted as she studied him. "You really do, don't you?"

He gently cupped her face in his hands, wishing he could pour every drop of his love for her into that tender touch. "I very much do, exactly as you are, exactly who you are. There is no one in this world more perfect for me than you. If you'll have me."

"Are you asking me to marry you?" Her voice caught.

In truth, he had prepared to ask her if she would allow him

to court her. But if she were willing to skip over the process and simply be his wife, he would take that over the former with great pleasure.

"Or should I say, are you proposing marriage…a second time?" she added playfully.

Lucian shrugged. "I presume as it worked so efficaciously for Mr. Darcy, so, too, might it fall in my favor."

"You read the books," Hannah said with what appeared to be genuine surprise.

"All three volumes." Lucian nodded. "I dare say that while it was no *Odyssey*, it was well written and far more engaging than I anticipated. I'm glad to have been introduced to such compelling works that I might never have known otherwise. In this and so many other ways, you have made me a better man."

HANNAH'S HEART nearly burst at the realization that Lucien had not only read *Pride and Prejudice* but that he'd managed to work it into his proposal.

He must honestly love her if he had tolerated the awfulness of Lady Alison for a full fortnight on her behalf.

"Oh, Lucien." She grasped his hand and held it as though he were the only thing tethering her to the earth. "You needed no improvement."

He chortled. "I absolutely did."

"But you didn't," she protested. "I loved the way your old clothes fit you and how your hair was slightly too long." She reached for his cropped hair with her free hand. It was as silky beneath her fingertips as she'd imagined it would be.

"You were perfect as you were with your sweet charm and your unpolished candor."

His cheeks colored in the glow of light washing over them from the ballroom. "You liked me how I was?"

"Yes." Her heart pounded in a way she never thought it would. "And I love you too."

A wide grin spread over his handsome face. "Do you?"

"I have for some time, but I've been so afraid of rejection that I let it drive a wedge between us. I wanted to prevent myself from getting hurt." She took a deep breath. "I didn't think it was possible for anyone to love me. It's why I had the pact with the other ladies."

"The pact?"

Hannah clapped her hands over her mouth in horror at what she'd shared.

Lucien's brow quirked up. "Oh, now I must know."

Hannah gave a resigned sigh and shook her head. "It was a pact never to wed that the other ladies and I signed when we were at Lady Finch's Finishing School. We had plans to live in a manor in the country together, free to do whatever we wanted without judgment." She rattled off the list they each had and how greatly they longed for the freedom to pursue what they enjoyed the most.

"I can see the appeal to that," Lucien nodded. "But while I hate to ruin your plans..." He knelt before her and held her hand in his.

Her pulse spiked as she knew exactly what was coming.

"Hannah Bexley, you are the most beautiful woman in the world to me, and you've lit my life in ways I never knew possible." His gaze met hers and held it with earnestness as he spoke. "Would you do me the esteemed honor…in front of our eager audience…"

He glanced to the window where all four of her friends' faces were plastered against the glass, watching them. Hannah and Lucien shared a laugh before he continued, "Will you become my wife?"

She nodded enthusiastically. "Yes," she gasped. "Yes! Nothing would make me happier."

"Not even a manor in the country for you and your friends?" he asked with a grin as he straightened.

"Not even that." She threw her arms around his shoulders, and he kissed her soundly.

A click sounded, and the door to the ballroom was thrown open amid the excited squeals of her friends.

A figure approached from behind them, and the excitement bubbling through Hannah diminished somewhat.

Lady Brightstone.

Her posture was severely rigid, her head held at a proud angle. "I owe you an apology, Miss Bexley."

Hannah said nothing as the hurtful things the other woman had said welled in her anew.

"Lady Arksford told me after the fact that she knew you were in the bushes at Vauxhall Gardens. I realized then you'd heard what I said." The muscles in her neck strained as she drew in a deep inhale. "I was immediately ashamed and tried to defend it with false means. My son is a strong man with a sense of justice. When he told me I needed to examine my own life, I realized exactly why I was so ashamed of how I'd spoken of you and how very wrong I was. He had defended you from my unfair accusations from the first."

Her gaze went first to Lucien and then back to Hannah.

"You are a good woman, Miss Bexley. If he asked you to marry him, I truly hope you said yes."

"I did." Hannah nodded, unable to trust herself to say anything more. Not with her throat so tight with the force of her surging emotions.

All the dreams she had once been too scared even to hope to wish for had finally come true in the most beautiful way. She had found love.

16

JULY 12, 1816, SKIPTON, ENGLAND

By Hannah's request, she and Lucien opted for a four-month engagement. Not because she didn't wish to wed him straight away, for she most ardently did. In part, because she wanted to leave room in case he changed his mind, but also because her idea of a dream wedding was not at St. George's Church. She wanted summer flowers draped over arches and dripping from the polished wooden pews at the small chapel in Skipton.

Not only did Lucien not change his mind about marrying her, but he was elated at the idea of having the wedding in the country instead of under the prying eyes of the ton.

Hannah's friends all congregated at Westwich Manor in Skipton immediately after the season ended, and the morning of her wedding finally arrived. The ladies dashed about the room this way and that, in a flurry of activity with maids running into one another in an attempt to get them all into dresses and have their hair perfectly styled. But amid that flurry came a barrage of laughter and good cheer.

After all, the first of Lady Finch's ladies who had vowed never to wed was actually getting married.

"So what did you tell Lady Alison?" Elizabeth queried while her maid pinned several rosettes into a loose, upswept hairstyle.

They all looked to Lucy, who had insisted on being the one to quell Lady Alison's need to spread gossip about Hannah and Lucien's indiscretion.

Lucy feigned innocence. "What is said between ladies should remain between ladies." A cheeky smile curled her lips. "But be sure she will never speak ill of any of us for as long as she lives."

"You are so very wicked," Hannah laughed.

"Thank God," Jillian confirmed, and they all erupted into giggles.

"And how do you feel now that you're free?" Amy asked Jillian who the Duke of Dudley had abandoned in place of the affections of Lady Alison.

Jillian spread her arms wide and leaned her head back. "Free," she repeated with a sigh.

Lucy scowled as she smoothed her hand over her silky dark hair. "I do hate that she gets to marry a duke."

"You needn't worry," Elizabeth said confidently. "The villain of a story always pays the price."

Jillian barked a shrill laugh. "Perhaps her price is having to endure Dudley for the rest of her life."

"I believe you are finally ready, my lady." Mary ceased the little plucks and tucks of her primping and moved back to observe her work.

Tears filled Amy's eyes as she gazed at Hannah despite her

attempts to blink them away. "Oh, Hannah. You look every bit what a bride should be."

"Are you crying?" Lucy teased.

"Wait until the wedding," Elizabeth said. "I believe we will all require a handkerchief to witness our amazing Hannah marrying the man she loves." She nudged Lucy with her elbow. "Even you."

Lucy discreetly pulled a delicate handkerchief from her sleeve to demonstrate. "I'm fully prepared."

Jillian waved Hannah forward. "Come see how beautiful you look."

They all turned to Hannah as she strode toward the mirror, breathe held, body tense.

While Hannah had always liked her eyes for the way they reminded her of her father, and even her hair on occasion for how different it was from everyone else's, she'd never considered herself anything above pretty on her good days. Plain on most others. But at that moment, gazing at the mirror on the wall, she truly did feel beautiful.

Her hair was lifted from her shoulders amid a crown of pale pink roses with sprays of small white flowers, and her mother's diamonds shone at her throat. The gown, made by Madame Bannery while they were still in London, was simple blue silk with dozens of tiny crystals sewn into the bodice to represent the constellations, so she glittered like the night sky when she walked in the day.

Her friends were not the only ones to have need of a handkerchief. Hannah blinked back her tears, and immediately, four handkerchiefs were thrust in her direction. She waved them all off with a laugh and turned from the mirror. "I have something from Lucien that he said I must open prior to our arrival at the chapel."

Mary hastened over, holding an envelope from Lucien. "I'll send for the carriage," she said as she passed the item to Hannah.

But before she could rush out, Hannah caught her maid's hand and squeezed it affectionately. "Thank you for everything."

After all, Mary had done so much more for Hannah than always being at her side. She had persisted with Lord Brightstone even after Hannah had given up. It was to Mary whom Hannah owed her happiness.

Mary had always had a gift for getting others to trust her, and in only a few intentional run-ins with the Brightstone staff at market, she was well aware of how miserable Lucien was with Lady Alison. A few convincing chats with Lucien's valet and she had discovered the truth, information Lucien's valet shared in the hopes Mary could mend what was broken.

And mend it she did, with the help of Hannah's closest friends when Hannah had stubbornly refused to listen.

"I would do it all again in a heartbeat to see you this happy, dearest Hannah." Mary embraced her charge and then shooed the other maids from the room as she departed.

Hannah wiped a tear from her eye, sniffed and faced her friends with her emotions solidly restored once more. "Lucien said this gift was something he wanted me to open in front of you all. He worried after the wedding we might be too excited and forget, but conveyed that it was very important."

"I'm intrigued." Elizabeth rubbed her hands together eagerly.

"Me too." Hannah broke the seal on the envelope and extracted a letter, leaving a folded item inside that appeared to be made of very thin paper. She unfolded the note and read it aloud.

"*My beautiful bride, you have made all my worldly wishes become a reality. This is perhaps the only way I can think to repay you—by making one of your worldly wishes become a reality as well.*"

Elizabeth gave a little squeal and kicked her feet in excitement.

"*I imagine a fortnight or so several times a year for you and your friends will be a delightful reprieve from daily life. Please note that the kitchen will be fully stocked with whatever Miss Honeyfield may require.*"

Hannah looked up at her friends in surprise at the curious statement.

"*An art room has been prepared for Lady Jillian. A music room has been equipped with a commendable number of instruments for Miss Beauchamp and a library filled with novels like* Pride and Prejudice *for Lady Elizabeth. There is also a phaeton for you, my love, to spirit through the countryside.*" Hannah cried out the word "phaeton," never having dreamed she might own such a swift, fine carriage.

"*Thank you to your friends for sharing you with me. The least I can do is return the favor. I am forever in their debt.*"

With the final sentence read, Hannah pulled the folded item from the envelope. The deed to Rosewood Manor, located near Kent, was written in the name of Hannah Lambert.

In addition to a lifetime of love and happiness, Lucien had also given Hannah her manor with her friends, a place for them to go and always be themselves. Though something told

Hannah that she would never again have to be anyone she wasn't when it came to her husband.

The women stared at one another in stunned silence at the enormity and consideration of such a gift.

"He has certainly made breaking the pact worthwhile," Hannah said with a wide grin as her friends rushed forward to embrace her.

A knock sounded at the door, and Mary entered. "My lady, the carriage is ready."

Hannah stood straight and tall, her heart so full she wondered how it could fit in her chest. "And I am too."

THERE WAS no doubt in Lucien's mind that Hannah enjoyed her gift. Upon the arrival of her carriage, she and her friends erupted into the sunlit morning and raced toward him with excited squeals and a cacophony of gratitude.

"I thought I wasn't supposed to see you in your gown before you walked down the aisle." He grinned and gazed at the stunning woman who was to become his wife.

"The whole point of the country is that we get to make our own rules and be out of the eyes of those who would judge us." She slowly turned to show off her gown.

But it wasn't satin and muslin that his eyes feasted upon. It was the narrow waist, the sweep of her red hair off her long, graceful neck and the fullness of her bosom. These months they held off marrying had been worth it to have the marriage of their choice, but other parts had not been so easy.

Stolen kisses in moments of brief privacy, no matter how passionate they might be, only served to whet his ever-growing appetite for his soon-to-be wife. He wanted to grab her by her tiny waist and draw her against the wall of his body, to make her cry out with pleasure as she had done that time at Vauxhall Gardens.

She slipped into his dreams and lingered in his thoughts through the day. Finally, once they had properly celebrated their wedding, she would be his.

As she faced him once more, the glittering of crystals on her gown seemed inconsistent—as random as the stars. He studied them a moment, pointing to three gems placed in an evenly spaced line. "Is that…"

"Orion's belt." Hannah beamed at him. "It is. Almost all the constellations are there."

And they were, the gems winking in a perfect mirror of the night sky.

"Do you like it?" Hannah asked with a smile, knowing full well he would.

"I love it." He caught her by the waist and spun her about, pausing to kiss her. "And I love you."

Someone cleared their throat. He glanced over to where Hannah's maid watched them sternly. "Oh, come now, Mary," he beseeched.

She lifted her nose in the air. "No more kisses until you marry her, my lord."

Lucien winked at Hannah. "It seems there's nothing for it but to make you my wife." He offered her his arm. "Shall we?"

She accepted. "We shall."

He led her to the small church and deposited her with Lord Westwich before going inside to wait by the altar for Hannah.

"I thought he wasn't supposed to see you yet," Lord Westwich protested as Lucien strode away, followed by Hannah's beautiful laugh.

The nave was exactly as Hannah had described she wanted it, adorned with summer flowers that had managed to withstand the abnormally chilly summer—pink roses that matched the sweet crown at her head and with daisies, bright violets and creamy yellow buttercups. The heady floral perfume masked the musty old familiar scent Lucien was so aware of in the old church and lent a newness that seemed fitting for their fresh start together as a married couple.

The ceremony was brief, the vicar getting as emotional as Hannah's friends and mother when he wed the two people he had known since childhood. A sniff behind Lucien had him glimpsing over his shoulder to catch his mother dabbing at her eyes.

Ranford, who had said he wouldn't dream of missing the event, sat at her side and nodded with encouragement.

"I now pronounce you," the vicar announced, his chin trembling, "Man and wife."

Lucien grinned at Hannah and pulled her close, gently capturing her mouth with his. A cheer rose from their audience; the scant number of attendees did not mean the collective cry of celebration was any less deafening.

The wedding breakfast was served in the dining room of Lambert Abbey. Though Lucien's mother—now the Dowager Countess of Brightstone—had never been one to lavish the house with flowers, the formal dining area was laden with them amid plates of sliced meats and cheese, various soups and fruits and a lovely cake sprinkled with glittering sugar crystals that Hannah confessed had been made by Miss Honeyfield.

"I told Hannah this would be so romantic, right from the very beginning, didn't I, Mary?" Lady Westwich beamed at Hannah's maid.

"Yes, my lady," Mary smiled back as she wiped a tear from her eye. "You did."

"I knew you would marry a man who loves you as you are, in all your perfection." Lord Westwich embraced Hannah and then slid a warning look in Lucien's direction as if to confirm the discussion earlier would be remembered.

And how could Lucien ever forget the list of bodily harm the baron would shamelessly exact upon Lucien's person should he ever dream of harming Hannah again?

Lucien nodded at Lord Westwich in understanding, then was surprised when the older man hugged him as well. "That look in my daughter's eye..." Westwich nodded to Hannah, who watched them both with the radiance of sheer joy. "You put that there." He squeezed Lucien's shoulder and went on his way.

"It appears she has done the same to my son." Lucien's mother looked between them and smiled. The expression was still stiff, as though being newly stretched out after so little use. "Now, let us eat this lovely feast that has been laid before us."

The invitation bordered on formal, but it was also far warmer than the countess would ordinarily address people. She was not perfect, sometimes sliding back into her judgmental habits, but she was trying. And for that, Lucien was grateful.

Everyone moved to secure a plate, except Lucien, who hung back with Hannah.

"What did my father say to you?" she asked. "I saw that look."

Lucien took her hand in his. "Nothing we need ever worry about because I would rather die a thousand deaths before I ever hurt you again."

"And if not, he would do the task for you?" Hannah surmised.

"Something along those lines, yes." He kissed her hand.

She studied him, gazing into his eyes. "I love you so very much, husband."

"I love you as well, my beautiful wife."

"Do not think me appallingly wicked..." She glanced toward the wedding party descending on the table of food. "But how long do you think it will take them all to finally leave?"

"Oh, I do think you appallingly wicked." He grinned. "And I was wondering precisely the same thing."

17

Once everyone had eaten their fill and not even a crumb of Amy's decadent cake remained, they took their leave and Hannah and Lucien were finally alone.

Fully and completely alone.

The dowager countess departed to visit with Lady Arksford for a week, and even the staff had been given the day off to celebrate the wedding. After all, she and Lucien could fare for themselves with the leftover food from the wedding breakfast.

He reached for her in the drawing room where they'd bid their servants a good day, but she shook her head. "Not here."

"No one is here but us." He leaned forward, bringing with him the scent of shaving soap and books and that sensual masculine spice of his.

But she leaned away, breathless with anticipation. "If I kiss you now, I don't think I'll ever stop."

"Then why are we standing here?" He swept her into his arms and carried her up the flight of stairs as if she weighed almost nothing.

"Aren't I heavy?" she asked, laughing.

"Not at all." He wasn't even out of breath.

He nudged open the door to a massive room with polished mahogany furnishings and heavy blue velvet. There was a familiar scent to the room that made it smell completely and intimately like her husband.

"I hope it was all right to bring you to my room." He set her gently to the ground and looked around with a sheepish grin. "I thought perhaps we might share the chamber, rather than have separate beds." With a small half-shrug, he added, "since we are doing what we want rather than abiding by tradition."

"I love that idea." She stared up at him, her handsome husband with blond waves slightly too long to be fashionable. With poignance, she reached up and swept his hair from his eyes, reveling in the silky feel.

Finally, she could kiss him, touch him, experience him in the entirety that her body had ached for in the last few months. Memories of how he had touched her at Vauxhall Gardens seared her mind and played out in her thoughts constantly.

A low pulse of hot temptation thudded to life between her thighs. In an eye-opening and confidential chat with Lucy, Hannah had been told how she could slake such desires. The way Lucien had done that one night amid the popping fireworks. But Hannah had held off, wanting to share the experience of her releases with Lucien.

"I have waited so long for his moment," he said, his ragged voice snagged at a primal part of her. One that desired him as desperately as he so obviously desired her.

His hands skimmed down her dress, brushing the sides of

her breasts and resting at her narrow waist. With a groan, he drew her body against the length of him. Already the hardness of what her mother had called "his manness" nudged low at her belly.

Lucy had called it a "prick" and a "cock" interchangeably. Those words appealed to Hannah far more. They felt more mature. More desirable. Something she wanted to take into her hand, as Lucy had mentioned.

Hannah's heart thundered in her ears as her mother's advice tangled with Lucy's whispered giggles. It would hurt the first time. It would be the most divine sensation in the world. One mustn't completely disrobe if one did not desire to. If he were a true lover, he would lick her like a treat.

Heat scorched through her body on that last bit, as Lucy had pointed to the excerpt in a well-handled pamphlet with a satisfied smirk.

"I don't know what to do," Hannah whispered.

"Whatever you wish." Lucien smiled patiently at her and caressed her cheek, then her throat and over the swell of her breasts where her skin was suddenly exquisitely sensitive.

"Whatever feels good." His eyes followed the path of his hand. "There is no wrong way unless it is something you do not wish."

A shuddering exhale escaped her. There was nothing she wanted omitted. She wanted all of what loving entailed in that instant. Starting with a kiss she knew would ignite into so much more.

She rose onto her toes as she closed her eyes, her chin tilting toward him. He caught the back of her head in his large hands and kissed her, his lips whispering over hers, his tongue sweeping into her mouth.

Her moan was quiet at first in the recesses of her throat, but when he cupped her bottom and angled her pelvis against his, so his prick pressed more firmly against her, the sounds coming from her did not remain quiet.

With no one about in the massive house, there was no need to stifle their enjoyment. If it felt good, she would openly moan and scream as she so chose. The idea was liberating.

She gasped in delight and met his tongue with her own, eager to fulfill the yearning that burned through her for what felt like an eternity.

He rested his forehead against hers, panting. "I've wanted you for so long, Hannah. From that first moment that I saw you in the field last January."

"Was it my grace?" she laughed.

"It was your beauty, your heart and the goodness to save a cat." He grinned. "And it might have had something to do with a bare, shapely leg with a fallen stocking."

"You are wicked," she accused with a mock look of outrage. "You were not supposed to look."

"I am wicked," he said raggedly. "And I want you as I have never wanted anything."

"Then you may have me." She put her hands to his chest, her fingers trembling. "All of me."

With a tentative glance up at him, she undid the buttons of his jacket, so it gaped open, then pushed it from his shoulders. He'd returned to wearing his looser garments, but for their wedding, he wore a fitted suit that displayed his fine body.

He reached for her, carefully plucking the pins from her hair and letting them drop in muted plops against the carpet until her red tresses tumbled around her. "Beautiful." He studied her. "So beautiful."

Then, without another word, he lowered his mouth to hers again and kissed her with the passion she had been craving. Their lips slanted against one another in desperation, their tongues mating. He nudged his knee between her legs, so his strong thigh rested exactly where the pulse of her desire flared brightest.

She moaned as pleasure coursed through her in a way that eased and encouraged her lust at the same time.

His fingers moved behind her, unbuttoning the row of small buttons down her back. It must have been a maddening process, but he never grew irritated. Instead, for every button he popped free, he paused to caress the newly exposed skin with his fingertip, savoring the undressing of her.

At that moment, she knew she wanted to fully disrobe for him, for him to lovingly stroke every part of her in such a reverent manner. And she wanted the same of him. As luxurious as it was to experience their hands on one another's skin, she could only imagine the touch of their naked bodies, hot and delightfully sensitive together.

The bodice of her gown widened and slid from Hannah's shoulders before pooling in a stiff pile on the ground. She stepped from it even as he reached for the bow at her chemise. Her nipples thrust out from the shapeless garment, hard-tipped and rosy-pink beneath the thin fabric.

He groaned and bent over her, drawing one bud into his mouth through the thin cloth, the heat of his tongue flicking against it.

If he were a true lover, he would lick her like a treat.

Hannah cried out and cradled his head to her bosom, understanding now what the pamphlet meant. At some point, he managed to lift away her chemise, though, for the life of her, she could not recall precisely when that had happened. Somewhere between the time he cupped her other breast and loved it with his mouth, the fabric miraculously slipped away.

Whatever strength once held up her legs seemed to dissolve, and she felt herself leaning heavily on him. But he did not falter, his body as strong as a block of stone.

It was then his fingers trailed lower on her body, from the dip of her navel to tease over the thatch of fiery hair between her thighs. He swept his delicious touch between her thighs, and that familiar pleasure from the Vauxhall fireworks jolted through her. The strength of her knees bled away, and she nearly sagged against him.

"You're so wet, Hannah." He secured her against his strong body. "God, I want you so desperately."

"Take me," she whispered. "Slake this fever you set in me."

Lifting her into his arms once more, he carried her to the great bed where he lay her upon the plush blanket, impossibly soft beneath her skin. His gaze lingered on her, taking her in as his fingers worked down the buttons of his waistcoat before shrugging it off. Next came the cravat he unwound from his neck, tied in a Mail Coach Knot, she noticed with a smile. The same as it had been since she'd made the suggestion.

He drew up the hem of his shirt, revealing a rigid band of abdominal muscles that flexed as the fabric slowly unveiled the rest of his powerful torso. Hannah's mouth went dry.

The only bare chest Hannah had ever seen in her life was that of the stablehand with Lady Alison, and he looked nowhere near as...chiseled as Lucien. He met her gawking stare with a shy smile.

She sat up and reached for him, bringing him toward her,

eager to feel the firmness of his hard body against the softness of hers. The sprinkle of hairs at his strong chest rasped against her nipples as he pressed against her, capturing her lips once more.

Now. She wanted him now. Her body writhed beneath him as she parted her thighs to cradle the weight of his body. The silky, hot length of his cock rested over her entrance, and she ground against him in anticipation.

But he did not push into her as the pamphlet said he would. Instead, he kissed her one final time before crawling off her. He did not remove his breeches. Instead, he knelt at the end of the bed where her legs were still slightly parted. His fingers grazed her knees, her thighs, the tender area just before the cleft between her thighs.

A whimper of longing escaped her, eager for the play of his dexterous fingers over her most intimate area.

He leaned over her, his face nearing the cleft between her legs and, watching her, he ran his tongue along the seam of her sex. Pleasure shot through her, stunning her for a moment. Her body acted on instinct and she gripped the blanket as he licked at her once more.

If he were a true lover, he would lick her like a treat.

Heavens! That was what the pamphlet meant.

The sensation was incomparable to anything she had ever experienced, even the stroke of his fingers there. Her entire self prickled with overly heightened nerves, her nipples taut, her breath coming in gasps though she simply lay there, her legs trembling as they strained open against his ministrations.

Something nudged at her center while his tongue wrought the most thrilling delight. She glanced at him as he gently inserted his finger into her entrance, and she moaned, loud and shameless.

"I want you," she said in a breathy plea. "Please."

"Not yet," he murmured as he continued to love her with his mouth and hand.

A tingling sensation wound through her, and a familiar tightness wound through her core. Lucien must have noticed the change in her as well, for his tongue flicked faster, his finger plunging as he tilted her over the edge of the decadent precipice.

Pleasure exploded through her, like the fireworks of Vauxhall Gardens all over again. She cried out, more of a scream if she were being honest, and she didn't care. Only the pleasure mattered.

Her body trembled with the power of what had wracked through her, and yet that need for Lucien was even more insistent now. One she didn't entirely understand despite her talk with her mother and with Lucy, but one she knew she could not deny.

Lucien stood once more, his gaze bright with desire beneath his shaggy blond hair. His hands went to his breeches and unbuttoned the fall. Brazenly, Hannah let her stare slide down his carved torso to his cock jutting from his body, hard as her mother had said they became.

Hannah swallowed.

He stepped tentatively toward her as if he was worried that he might frighten her, and shifted over her once more. But he still didn't immediately attempt to shove inside her. No, he nuzzled against her, kissing first her neck and under her ear, and then capturing her lips until she was squirming beneath him with eager longing.

His hard heat pressed against her sex, and she cried out in anticipation.

Now, finally, he would fulfill what she had been longing for. Now, she would fully be his wife.

LUCIEN HOVERED over Hannah for what felt like an eternity. His prick was so swollen that it bordered on painful. Never had he realized he could be brought to the point of such need.

No matter how insistently his desire urged him to claim her hard and fast, he continued to glide his hands over her smooth skin to coax her body into an extreme state of arousal. He ought to have stopped earlier before her climax, so her longing was at its peak.

Except when he felt that telltale tensing of her muscles, he had known he couldn't draw away. And he was glad he didn't —the huskiness of her cries still echoed sweetly in his ears. He had brought her great pleasure, and he would never regret that.

Only now, he hoped he did not bring her great pain.

Hannah's fingers roamed over him as they kissed and teased one another. Her touch traced over the lines of his body with an appreciation that made him proud of the efforts with his body. He had studied philosophy for a good part of his life, and a healthy body was always touted in tandem with a healthy mind. The rigorous routine of daily calisthenics had always been to keep his health in good standing, but now, seeing Hannah's reaction to him, his efforts would continue in the goal of pleasing his wife as well.

The pitch of her panting told him she was primed once

more. He propped himself on his right arm to keep from resting his body weight on her and angled his arousal against her entrance. Even the mere brush of the swollen head of his prick against her slick center was exquisite torment.

He flexed his hips forward, slowly, nudging inside her one careful thrust at a time. The pain and pleasure warred on Hannah's lovely face. He tried to stop, but she shook her head and arched up against him, ever the one to charge ahead.

His fingers shifted between them to find the little bud of her sex, rolling his fingertip around it. She gasped, and the tension squeezing his cock in an almost painful grip relaxed somewhat.

The next time he gently pushed into her, her lashes fluttered with pleasure. Yes, this was precisely what he had wanted.

She arched up to meet him on his next thrust, and he moved slightly faster. Her breathing shifted, becoming faster, shallower with her delight.

He continued to let his finger work over the sensitive nub while he drove harder into her. Hannah grabbed his shoulders, clinging on, and he knew she was close to her release.

The tightening of his ballocks told him she was not the only one.

It was all he could do to ensure she reached her climax first. But he refused to allow himself to be pleased if she had not been.

He entered her with quick, deep strokes, and she moaned in pleasure against his ear until at last, her body went tight, and her sex squeezed at him, drawing him to orgasm as they both cried out. The power of his release tore through him like something savage, and he yielded to its force, riding the waves that took him higher than ever before and then finally collapsing beside Hannah.

She lay there for a moment, gazing up at the ceiling, her breasts rising and falling as her breathing calmed. As an edge of worry crept over him, she turned her head toward him as a slow smile eased the corner of her mouth upward.

"That was…" She sighed and gave a long, slow blink. "The most remarkable thing in the world."

He pulled her into his arms, and she rested her head against his chest as if she were made to fit perfectly against him. "I was afraid I would hurt you."

"I expected something far worse based on my mother's discussion with me." Hannah giggled. "But then, she has always been one to overreact."

"I'm so glad you found it so pleasurable." Lucien traced his fingertips over Hannah's silky skin, awed by how smooth and soft she was. "There are so many more ways to share our bodies, and we have a lifetime to explore them together."

She nestled closer against him. "I eagerly anticipate trying them all."

And that was exactly how they spent a good amount of their time in the country. During the day, they rode through the countryside in bundled clothes against the chilly summer, warmed by companionship and love. But at night, he taught her about the stars in the night sky and together, they learned each other's bodies amid a tangle of sheets.

Never had anything in Lucien's life been more ideal. Never had he dreamed marriage could be like this. And he realized that through all the books on philosophy and the study of life, he'd finally learned the true meaning of happiness through Hannah.

EPILOGUE

FEBRUARY 1817, LONDON

Hannah rested one hand on her newly rounded stomach and reached for a tea cake with the other.

"Have you been feeling well?" Amy asked anxiously. "My mother was always dreadfully ill when with child."

Hannah smiled at Amy's kindness at always considering others. "In the first two months, I was quite unwell, but Lucien and his mother coddled me endlessly until I was feeling better. I've been fine these last two months."

"The Dowager Countess of Brightstone coddled you?" Lucy asked, incredulous.

Hannah smiled. "Well, in as much as she can. She has been surprisingly welcoming." From time to time, the older woman had a biting comment, but more often than not caught herself, apologized and restated her words in a softer, more civil manner. She was certainly trying, and Hannah would always appreciate the effort.

"I wonder if you'll have a boy or a girl." Jillian tilted her head to the side. "Either way, you're glowing with happiness."

231

"It almost makes one want to get married," Elizabeth said with a blush.

"Almost," Lucy muttered.

Which reminded Hannah. "Before tea concludes, I have something for you ladies." They had spent the last two hours laughing and catching up on what had transpired in their lives over summer. While Hannah giggled and declined to share all, hers had been idyllic; a dream she never had to wake from.

And while Hannah enjoyed the visit with her friends immensely, the weight of exhaustion was beginning to settle over her, a common occurrence since she'd realized her courses had ceased.

"Since I am no longer part of the pact…" She withdrew from behind a pillow the old leather-bound journal with green vines and blue flowers crawling over its edges.

Lucy arched a brow. "That looks familiar."

"Is that our shared diary from Lady Finch's?" Elizabeth asked.

"It is." Hannah presented it in the air with a flourish. She flipped through the pages, filled with five sets of handwriting and paused with a gasp. "Oh my, here is the day I stumbled upon Lady Alison in the stable. 'I followed a distinct squeaking sound, and much to my surprise…'"

They all erupted into laughter.

"Has anyone had word on Lady Alison?" Elizabeth asked.

Their focus shifted to Jillian.

"Of course, I would have news." Jillian shook her head wryly. "Very well. Last I heard, the duke intended to propose to Lady Alison, so I suppose we shall see. But in the meantime, my father has agreed to allow me a year to acquire a husband on my own before he throws me into another match."

Amy frowned empathetically. "But you don't want to wed."

Jillian sighed. "At least it is a year from his persistence to secure a husband for me."

"Or it could be the most romantic introduction to the man you love," Elizabeth said with delight.

"Elizabeth," they all cried in unison, which set her giggling.

Hannah held up the book. "Speaking of marriage, it seems only right to grant this to one of you in the hope it will bring you luck in breaking the pact."

"I don't want it." Jillian scooted back on the sofa, away from Hannah.

"Fate will decide." Hannah pulled four bits of paper from the book's cover, each folded in half, and spread them in her fingers like playing cards. "There are three stars and one heart. The heart wins."

Amy reached forward and plucked one from Hannah's fingers.

"Or loses," Lucy protested. "What if I don't want to play?"

Elizabeth took two and passed one to Lucy. "You don't have a choice."

Lucy scowled but still accepted the paper from Elizabeth as Hannah handed the last one to Jillian.

They all opened them together, and both Jillian and Lucy exhaled out a long sigh of relief.

"I suppose I'm to receive the book next," Elizabeth said softly. From her reaction, Hannah could not tell whether that pleased her or not.

"I hear Lord Darington is still perfectly available." Amy clapped her hands.

Elizabeth turned a strange shade of red. "Lord Darington would no sooner choose me for a wife than the queen would invite me to tea."

"I wouldn't say that." Lucy giggled. "Well, when you tried to mop up your lemonade, you did brush your handkerchief over his—"

"Lucy," Amy chastised.

Poor Elizabeth's face went entirely scarlet, and suddenly Hannah realized it might not have been the best idea to impose the suggestion of marriage with the passing of the book. After all, she had meant to share the concept that love was something grand to be had and that no one need alter their life based on a pact signed when they were still barely adults.

"What if he did ask to court you?" Jillian asked suddenly.

They all looked to Elizabeth and glanced down at the journal as she gently stroked its cover. "I don't believe I would decline him." She smiled shyly, and Hannah's fears were immediately quelled.

Hopefully, this book would bring her luck in love. As it had for her with Lucien.

She bid farewell to her friends, eager to join them the following evening at Lord and Lady Whimbly's ball to open yet another new season. With a tired sigh, Hannah knew it was time to yield to the beckoning of an afternoon rest.

As she climbed the curving staircase, she came upon Lucien's mother. "Are you well?" The dowager asked, concern crinkling her brow. "Perhaps your friends ought not have stayed so long."

"I'm well," Hannah said. "Simply a little tired, as I generally am in the afternoon. It was well worth the effort to visit with my friends again."

"Shall I have Mary fetch you some tea?"

"Perhaps afterward, but for now, I am content to rest a moment." Hannah touched her hand to her mother-in-law's forearm. "But thank you for the consideration."

The dowager nodded in understanding and departed with only one last backward glance. Initially, the older woman's perpetual fluttering about unsettled Hannah. Until Lucien had explained that his older brother died as an infant before Lucien was born.

Though the babe settled in Hannah's belly had months to grow before she could meet him or her, there was already a connection established, something that rooted deep in her heart. She could not imagine what her mother-in-law had endured with that loss and hoped never to experience such pain herself. But it gave her a stronger insight into her mother-in-law's actions and afforded Hannah more patience and understanding.

She opened the door to the bedroom she shared with Lucien and found him in a chair by the hearth with a book spread between his hands.

Immediately, he slid a bit of paper between the pages and closed the book, setting it aside. "I thought you might come here for a rest after your friends departed." He smiled at her, and her heart nearly melted in her chest.

"I cannot deny I am slightly more tired than usual." She met her husband halfway and kissed him.

He set his hand at her lower back, leading her toward their large bed. "Dare I ask who received the journal? I hope for your sake it wasn't Lady Jillian."

Hannah chuckled. "No, it was Elizabeth."

Lucien nodded. "Do you think she already has someone in mind?"

Hannah thought of the times Elizabeth had stolen glances at Lord Darington in the last year. "I think she does."

"Well, in that case, I wish her all the joy and happiness that we share together." Lucien put his arm around Hannah and gently rested his hand against the small bump that was beginning to swell at her lower stomach.

"I do too," Hannah agreed. Even as she said it, however, she could not help but recall how scandal trailed Lord Darington as a cat followed a fishmonger.

If he were truly meant for Elizabeth and they stood even a whisper of a chance, there would be a lot for them to overcome.

Perhaps more than Hannah and Lucien had had to face. She gazed at her husband now with a grateful smile.

"What is that look for?" he asked, his lips curling upward.

"For loving me for who I am."

"How could I not?" He pulled her into his arms and kissed her.

Once upon a time, she could have answered that question with a detailed list. But in the time that she'd known him, in the time he'd loved her, he had bestowed upon her so many notes of adoration, she no longer bothered to think back on such things.

He loved her thoroughly and completely for who she was, as she did him, and truly nothing in life could be more perfect. Except, of course, for soon being a family of three...and possibly more in the coming years. They were immensely happy together, and she wouldn't ever have it any other way.

And she fervently hoped her fellow wallflowers would be just as lucky.

Matchmaker of Mayfair

Discovering the Duke

Unmasking the Earl

Mesmerizing the Marquis

Earl of Benton

Earl of Oakhurst

Earl of Kendal

Heart of the Highlands

Deception of a Highlander

Possession of a Highlander

Enchantment of a Highlander

Standalones

The Highlander's Challenge - N W M S

Her Highland Beast - N W M S (fairytale twist retelling - Beauty and the Beast/Princess and the Pea with Scottish folklore)

ABOUT THE AUTHOR

Madeline Martin is a *New York Times, USA Today,* and International Bestselling author of historical fiction and historical romance with books that have been translated into over twenty different languages.

She lives in sunny Florida with her two daughters (known collectively as the minions), two incredibly spoiled cats and a man so wonderful he's been dubbed Mr. Awesome. She is a die-hard history lover who will happily lose herself in research any day. When she's not writing, researching or 'moming', you can find her spending time with her family at Disney or sneaking a couple spoonfuls of Nutella while laughing over cat videos. She also loves research and travel, attributing her fascination with history to having spent most of her childhood as an Army brat in Germany.

Check out her website for book club visits, reader guides for her historical fiction, upcoming events, book news and more: https://madelinemartin.com